RUBY & THE HUNTSMAN OF MIDNIGHT

SUSAN EE

WWW.SUSANEE.COM

Midnight Tales novels

Cinder & the Prince of Midnight

Ruby & the Huntsman of Midnight

Briar & the Dreamers of Midnight

Hansel & the Witch of Midnight

Don't miss a new story from Susan EE!

Sign up to hear about them at:

www. S u s a n E E .com

Aim your phone camera at this image to see the Midnight Tales novels

This is a work of fiction. All of the characters, organizations and events portrayed in this novel are either products of the author's imagination or used fictitiously. Any resemblance to actual persons, living or dead, or actual events is purely coincidental.

ISBN-13: 978-0-9835970-6-3

ISBN-10: 0-9835970-6-5

CHAPTER 1

*T*he dungeons of Midnight Castle were as bad as Ruby had heard. It was far below the sunshine and flowers of her grandmother's garden. Far below the decency of ordinary people. She had never heard of anyone escaping from here.

The only light came from the light of the moon. It slipped in between the slats on the ceiling of the corridor that split the rows of cells.

The walls were damp and the air was chilly. The dungeons were overcrowded, and they didn't care who they threw in together. A murderer could be thrown into the same cell with a child. A monster could be thrown in together with a victim of the Midnight Hunt.

It had been years since Ruby had been one of the human prey for the hunt, but she still considered herself one of the victims. That hunt had shaped her as much as her grandmother had.

She missed her family the most during the worst of times. She used to always be able to count on her grandmother to comfort and advise her. There had been far too many hard times for Ruby since she'd been taken from her family. And of all the nights she'd had to endure since the Midnight Hunt, this was likely going to be the worst.

Ruby was sure that the man in her cell was a monster.

They had thrown both of them in the dungeon on the night of the full moon. The entire castle was tense on the full moon, especially the survivors of the hunt. For them, there were always new surprises on those moonlit nights.

Guards had grabbed her out of her cot just after the moon rose and dragged her down the narrow corridors of Midnight Castle. No one ever explained what was about to happen on the full moon. She just had to brace herself for the worst.

They tossed her into the dungeon, along with the fresh crop of victims from last month's Midnight Hunt. Each of them were in their own cells. Like the others, Ruby held on to the bars of her cell to see if she could get a look at what she might have to face this night.

The cells were damp from the puddles of rain that had collected beneath the slats in the ceiling. Those openings let the rain and wind in, along with the beams of moonlight spearing the darkness. The dungeons had a particularly eerie feel with the sound of the anxious breathing of the prisoners as they all waited to see their fate.

Down the corridor, metal doors clanked, making Ruby clamp her hands tighter around the bars. Footsteps came down the stairs. A lot of them. Were they bringing in another group of prisoners?

The group walked through the beams of moonlight, breaking and warping the light as they strode down the corridor. These were no prisoners.

These men towered over the guards. At least, the ones in

the front did. Those were the ones who strutted with their bulging muscles. Some of them were naked. All of them were hairy, with tufts in the oddest places.

There was something strange about their lips, as though their mouths had been stuffed with bear traps. The moon lit only strips of them as they passed, so she couldn't get a good look. She could swear something glinted in their mouths, though. Whatever it was, it added to her unease.

Behind the first strutting giants, the others were shorter. No, not shorter. Stooped. Some of them were bent almost double so that their hands grazed the floor as they walked. Their heads jerked back and forth as if they heard noises that startled them.

One by one, the guards opened the cell doors, and one of these strange men walked into each cell.

Ruby backed away from the corridor. There was nowhere to hide in her small cell, but her instincts had her backing into the shadows anyway. Down the hall, the cell doors squeaked and clanked. Some of the prisoners began to cry in terrified, torn sobs that echoed down the hall.

Ruby's cell was one of the last. She squeezed as far away from the door as she could, trying to remember to breathe.

When her cell door opened, a stooped man walked into the cell without any shoving or threats from the guards. He wasn't chained, despite the fact that he was large and powerfully muscular.

He had cuts all over him. What really convinced her that he was a monster, though, was the blood.

There was blood all over his face. He had it on his chest and hands too.

Ruby knew a little about the ways that blood could splatter on a person. She'd learned them on her grandmother's lap as a little girl. This was an odd kind of blood pattern.

It told her that he had been the attacker and not the victim. But it hadn't been an ordinary fight.

An ordinary person would rarely use his mouth to attack.

CHAPTER 2

The hairy beast of a man paid no attention to Ruby. Instead, he curled on the rushes in the center of the cell. He groaned and twitched, sounding as though he was fighting pain or fury, or both.

Ruby got as far away from him as she could, huddling in the corner as she watched him.

Even her grandmother wouldn't be able to get her out of this. No one had ever escaped the Midnight dungeons before. It was infamous for its cruelty. And there were stories…

Ruby shut her eyes, willing away the old stories of what happened in the dungeons.

She stretched her neck, hearing the crackling and popping as though she was an old woman. She got up timidly, quietly, to move a little. She wanted to stay limber and ready, in case she needed to move quickly. The last thing she needed was to be stiff and clumsy if she had to run or fight.

She stretched her legs, loosening her tight muscles. The cell was cold and it was hard to warm up. All she wanted to do was sit silently as a mouse in the corner and hope he wouldn't notice her in the shadows. But hope could be a dangerous thing if it didn't come hand in hand with caution.

The man's breathing changed. He stopped twitching. Ruby had the feeling that he was watching her through his lashes.

A spike of panic washed over her. She was trapped in here with this man who had blood on his hands and face. His nails were tattered and clogged with something that looked like torn flesh.

This was only her first night in the dungeons, and she wasn't sure that she'd survive the night.

"I can defend myself." Ruby imitated her grandmother's voice—strong and full of confidence. "You'd be better off finding easier prey."

Of course, there was no easier prey than a girl trapped in a cell with a monster.

A low growl came from the man. A deep rumbling that was more animal than human.

Ruby forced herself away from the corner. The cell was small, but she was better off having space to maneuver. In the corner, she'd have nowhere to retreat to.

The man began twitching again on the floor the way a dog might twitch while dreaming. But he was awake, wasn't he?

Down the hall, someone screamed.

At the same time, there was a ferocious sound that was part growl and part animal screech.

Another scream.

This time, the sound was closer.

After that, the screams came in a wave down the corridor, as if whatever was happening was catching like fire from one cell to the next.

The man in Ruby's cell twitched and jerked. His face

contorted and his nose wrinkled. Then he screamed too. The sound was full of agony and violence.

The boy who was in the cell across the way grabbed the bars of his cell and screamed. He was no older than Ruby—old enough to be considered a man but young enough to sometimes be called a boy. He looked terrified and frantically tried to squeeze his way through the bars.

In the dark shadows beyond him, hairy hands reached out and grabbed him. His screams intensified, his eyes begging her for help. The hands dragged him back into the dark recesses of his cell.

All through the dungeon row, the air filled with screams and growls. The scariest sounds, though, were the screams that suddenly stopped midway. Or the screams that ended in a gurgle.

Despite Gran's old warnings about not backing herself into a corner, Ruby backed all the way against the wall.

The man in her cell jerked his head up. He led with his nose instead of his eyes, as if he was blind. But he clearly wasn't blind, because his eyes seemed to have an eerie yellowish glow as they watched her.

He dragged his weirdly long limbs as he pushed himself off the floor. Had they been that long before?

Despite his strange proportions, he moved gracefully without wasting a single motion. Like an animal. Like a predator.

Ruby heard herself pant. Her heart pounded in her ears, roaring panic raging through her.

Then the man—who was perhaps not entirely a man—curled his lips to show his unusually sharp teeth.

Before she could get out a scream, he leapt onto her.

CHAPTER 3

Tyler hated the stench of the dungeons. His grandfather would roll in his grave if he knew what the great Huntsman line had to do in order to keep their positions at Midnight Castle. They were hunters serving the royal family, not jailers. But these days, everyone who served the crown seemed to be a jailer.

He tried to ignore the stench and walked down the dingy corridor. The morning sun had finally come up and was streaming weakly through the slats in the ceiling.

He never came here in the dark. His superstitious resistance to come at night was probably a sign of his ancestors' low birth, but he didn't care. There was more to the world than what he could see and hear, and he was not foolish enough to ignore his instincts.

The night was getting longer, though, and each day got shorter. Soon, the sun would disappear altogether, according to the kitchen maids.

He walked down the corridor that split the rows of cells and looked into the carnage in each one. It wasn't that he wasn't used to seeing wild animals kill and feed; it was *what* they were feeding on that turned his stomach.

He tried to ignore the blood and bones, the gristle and head, the hair and fingers that were strewn about in the cells. He tried not to think about the angelic girl he'd caught a glimpse of before she was thrown into one of those cells. With large eyes and flame-colored hair, she had been the picture of vulnerability and fright.

Tyler had hardened himself to this job two years ago, when his father couldn't do the task anymore. He had to take over the job if he didn't want to anger the Dark King. Just being noticed by the king could be fatal—not just to the person catching the king's attention, but to his entire family.

As Tyler walked down the corridor, he occasionally stopped and pointed into a cell when he saw a specimen that he thought was ready. It took months for these beasts to fully transform, in theory. So far, they'd all failed, ending up with a yard full of what Tyler and his men called the howlers.

When Tyler pointed, his men went into the cell to carefully drag out the beast. It was a dangerous thing, this luring of monsters out of their den. It took six men for each one. A man with a net to throw over the beast. Two with long sticks with a noose at the end to tighten around its arms and neck. And two with barbed spears to coax it out of the dungeon.

They used to put the beasts directly into a cage, but then Tyler's men had to carry them up the stairs. That proved almost impossible to do with the monster thrashing about, tearing at the men. They'd only take the strongest of the litter, which made the whole ordeal even worse.

Tyler had been grateful he only had to do this horrible task two or three times a year. Lately, though, the Dark King had been going through his pets as though they were disposable game.

"Let's get this over with, lads. Then I'll buy you all a drink at the tavern tonight."

He'd seen the offer of a drink brighten up the boys in the past, but this was not a task that anybody would do if they had the choice—drink or not. Nor were they excited to have a drink with Tyler.

Although he still tried to maintain camaraderie with his men, he knew that he was no longer one of them. That was what happened when you went from the group's errand boy to their master.

Tyler picked out three beasts out of the dungeons. There were two more cells at the end of the row, but he only needed three. Any more and they'd be too hard to handle.

He was inclined to leave the last two cells without even looking at them. He was in no rush to add to the horror he'd already seen this morning. But his men were busy taking the last monster up the stairs, and Tyler couldn't get past them anyway.

So if he was stuck in the dungeons for a little while longer, he might as well inspect the last two creatures and see how they were faring. In the past, that would have been a pleasure for any of the animals he had been responsible for. He'd always had a deep connection with the animals under his care.

But the days of keeping stag and hare for the hunts were long gone. All he had left was this.

Tyler steeled himself for the carnage in the last two cells. He'd about reached his limit. The one to his right was like all the others. He tried to ignore the bloody mess and studied the beast coiled in the corner.

Did Tyler recognize the monster?

He turned away quickly in case it was someone he'd seen before. It was hard to tell with all the excess hair. Even their bone structure changed as the beast in them got stronger.

Nevertheless, he occasionally recognized someone. There was that baker six months ago, who used to sell him potato cakes. And the milkmaid who had actually been sweet on him for a week or two.

Tyler shook his head to get rid of the memories. This was a dark enough day as it was. He didn't need to invite more stains on his soul.

There was once a time when he was known as a friendly sort. But those days were long gone. These days, he didn't even want to look at a person's face unless they were part of his staff. He'd made them all a promise that if they turned into a beast, he'd end it for them quickly and not let it get this far. There would be no dungeons and chains for his men.

Only the last cell remained for him to look at. Unless this monster looked stronger and more aggressive than even the ones he'd already selected, Tyler would be done for the day.

What he saw there stopped his breath.

At first, he thought he'd lost his senses. He blinked, unable to take in what he was seeing. It took a moment, but eventually, he began to breathe again. His heart kept racing, though.

A slip of a girl sat in the cell.

The most noticeable thing about her was her deeply red hair. He couldn't tell if that was her natural color or if it was all the blood.

Unlike the other beasts, she'd squeezed herself into the corner as far away from her kill as she could. Her face, hands and ankles had no fur growing out of them, and that confused him. All the newborn howlers had fur growing on them by this point in their development.

She looked at him with dread in her eyes. She knew that he had power over her in the same way that a trapped rabbit knew.

Tyler frowned, arguing with his instincts. She couldn't be human. That wasn't possible.

The castle guards fed the transforming monsters small prey, like her. The king's sorcerers were obsessed with the idea that the beasts would complete a successful transformation if they ate a human sacrifice early in their development. It didn't matter that they hadn't had a single success yet. All they had were a yard full of howlers—neither men nor wolfkin.

Tyler took little comfort in the fact that the command had come directly from the Dark King. The king had instructed all of them personally in every detail of how the monsters should be raised and trained.

It killed Tyler a little each time when it was time to collect the new beasts from the dungeon for the king's menagerie. It had happened enough now that he was dead inside many times over. There had been some relief in that. A dead man had no heart to stir, no tears to pool, no loss of sleep over the death of so many of the kingdom's helpless citizens.

But now, the heart that Tyler was so sure he no longer had was calling for attention. It skipped beats, then raced at what he was seeing.

This was no beast looking back at him from the other side of the bars.

On the far side of the cell, the creature that should have torn her to pieces and eaten her was lying unmoving in the rushes.

It hadn't been an easy death for him. His head lay at an unnatural angle, as did his elbow and knee. One of his eyes was gouged out and hanging on his cheek.

Tyler looked back at the traumatized girl cringing in the corner of the cell. On closer inspection, she wasn't a child, although she gave the impression of one. She wasn't quite a full-grown woman yet, either. But she was thin and looked as weak as a piece of cloth.

"Did you kill him?"

His question was genuine. There had been no one else in the cell, but it was hard to fathom that this girl had fought off a monster.

Of course, this hadn't been a true monster like the wolfkin. They were mere imitations conjured up by the king's sorcerers, and only a few days old at that. Most of them wouldn't even survive the upcoming weeks, and so far, all of them had gotten stuck as a twisted howler that was not quite man, yet not quite wolfkin either.

Nevertheless, a howler was still a killer. They weren't as strong as wolfkin, but some might argue that they were just as savage. They were all instinct with no control—confused and dangerously insane for months to come.

He expected the girl to simper and cower, to not have enough courage to answer him. She seemed all eyes and vulnerability as she trembled there like a piece of fluff in the corner.

But she did answer him, and with a voice that didn't have the slightest tremor.

"Yes. I killed him."

CHAPTER 4

*R*uby hardly knew what was happening and didn't much care. She'd thought that the night she was captured had been the worst of her life, but last night had far exceeded it. She felt numb as the jailer opened her cell door and motioned for her to step out.

A part of her noticed that he was not dressed in the uniform of the others who had thrown her in here. He was dressed in suede and hard leather and carried a bow across his back, as if he was going out for a hunt.

Gran's lessons were so ingrained in her that she automatically noted the knives he carried—two at his waist, one in his boot. She had to assume that a man with this many weapons carried more that she couldn't see. Could she get one away from him?

He didn't seem particularly cautious, but he kept a close eye on her as she walked by him. He was much bigger than her, and she was so exhausted that she could barely stand. Whatever he wanted with her, she couldn't stop him.

"How did you do it?" asked the hunter.

"He attacked me." Her lips were so dry that she could barely get the words out.

"How did you kill him?"

He pointed to the stairs at the far side of the dungeon. That was the way out. Would they send her back out into the hunt for sport? Would they hang her in public for defending herself against whatever it was that they'd thrown into her cell?

"My grandmother taught me to fight." She shuffled down the aisle.

Ruby had been dreaming of her grandmother lately. It was strange yet comforting. In her dreams, Ruby continued her training with Gran, learning new moves and tactics that were useful in her real life. Of course, they must have been lessons that Gran had given her already that she was remembering through dreams, but they were remarkably useful.

"Ah, your grandmother was in the war."

Ruby nodded, staring at the cells as they walked by. She almost stumbled when she saw the carnage inside the cells.

Most of it was in the shadows, but she caught enough of the blood and gore to understand what had happened there. To understand that she was supposed to meet that same fate. It turned her stomach, but she'd already thrown up everything in it, so all it could do was heave.

She backed away from one cell, only to realize that she was getting too close to another.

"Are you frightened?" He sounded genuinely curious.

She looked sharply at him. "Why bother to torture? Why not just kill us outright and leave us some dignity?"

"Dignity?" He looked surprised. "The Dark King does not tolerate dignity in his kingdom. Don't you know that by now?"

Was that an insult to the king? If so, that bordered on treason.

15

But Ruby was just a country girl, not schooled in the ways of the court. Her grandmother had told her to never trust anyone from the castle. Gran worked with nobles all the time, and she was careful not to let Ruby weave fanciful notions around them. Romantic notions would get a girl killed, she'd always said.

Ruby wanted to be strong. *Needed* to be strong to survive this. The problem was that she wasn't all that strong. She was thirsty and hungry, and her legs trembled so much that she couldn't believe she'd walked this far. Her hands shook too.

Her mind kept screaming about the events that happened last night. How she was sure she would die. How she knew that unless she did horrible things to survive, those same horrible things would be done to her.

Ruby stumbled. The hunter jerked forward as if to catch her, but then he stopped and let her fall or not as she would. It was a curious motion, as if he hadn't quite made up his mind about what kind of a person he was.

She managed to stay on her feet. She kept her eyes straight ahead so that she wouldn't see the horror show in the cells on either side of her. When she reached the bottom of the stairs, though, the last of her strength ran out.

The stairs seemed to go up forever.

At the top, there was a sliver of light. It was sunshine, she was sure of it. Just the thought of feeling the warmth of the sun renewed her strength. She thought she'd never see it again.

She managed a few steps, but each step became harder to climb.

"I will *not* catch you if you fall," said the hunter.

She didn't say anything to that. Her grandmother would have made a sharp retort, but Ruby wasn't her grandmother.

She just climbed the next step. She kept expecting the

hunter to shove her up the stairs, but he waited and let her go at her pace.

Then she stumbled and fell to her knees. The pain was sharp and shot all the way up to her head.

She tried to get up, knowing that they would either kick her down the steps and watch her tumble or, if she was lucky, drag her up by her hair. But she was more exhausted than she'd ever been. She'd fought all night to stay alive, and that had taken more than she had.

She couldn't get up. Ruby would have cried then if not for the training of her grandmother. As a child, she'd rarely gotten any attention for crying. Gran had no time for silly things like that, so it had been trained out of Ruby at a young age.

The hunter called over his men. They looked like workers, while the hunter looked like a lord compared to them.

"Take her up and put her in a cage. Don't hurt her." He looked down at her with cautious eyes. "But don't let her looks fool you. Give her an opening, and she'll tear you to pieces like any of the other predators."

CHAPTER 5

*T*he girl wasn't a monster. Tyler wasn't sure what she was, but she wasn't a howler. He'd seen the whole life span of a howler, from the ways they could be born to the ways they could die. And this was no howler or wolfkin that he'd ever seen.

From what he could tell, she was just an exhausted young woman barely out of her girlhood. If he'd seen her out on the street, he would have dismissed her as weak and ordinary, maybe even timid.

She didn't resist when his men threw a net over her and cinched their ropes around her neck and body.

"Don't hurt her." His voice came out with as much command as the Dark King's. "She's fragile."

He stopped himself from saying that she was precious. He almost laughed at himself over the impulse. Nothing in Midnight could become precious to a person, not if he wanted to live.

That kind of weakness became a death sentence or a life of slavery as soon as someone found out about it, especially if that someone was from the court. Tyler already had his father, and far too many knew about that weakness.

Of course, he only meant that she was precious in the same way as a prized animal was precious. Better not to ever say the word in the first place, though, just in case someone misinterpreted his meaning.

His men could tell that he thought of her as special anyway. They must have known themselves that this girl was different. They'd pulled up plenty of predators from the dungeon, and none were anything like her.

More than a few crossed themselves in the manner of the old religion when they saw her. It took some courage to do it in the open, considering that the Dark King and most of Midnight was far from any religion. But they were men who handled the worst of the Dark King's creatures. Most people would forgive them for small trespasses like this, simply because they knew that no one would have taken this job unless they had no other choice.

They carefully and awkwardly picked up the girl and walked her up the stairs. They held their spears at the ready while carrying her by her shoulder and feet. She was wrapped in the net and ropes, and she seemed to be almost relieved to be off her feet.

He didn't like the way she slumped. She didn't even struggle. Her eyes were still open, but it looked like she was fighting to keep them that way.

Tyler could feel the threat of disappointment hanging over him. He had been so careful to manage his expectations that it was almost a surprise to feel it. It had been a long time since he'd had this level of interest.

He wanted to see what she was. What she could do. To see if she was an ordinary human or perhaps something more special.

There must have been plenty of other types of night creatures in the world that people didn't know about other than wolfkin, wraith horses, wild fairies, trolls and such. Perhaps she was something like that. Could a mere girl kill a wolfkin-like creature made from dark magic?

Possible. But it would take someone skilled, and even then, it would take luck in a tight dungeon cell. He could only find out if he kept her alive.

His men placed her in a cage and secured it with a heavy lock. The cage was his own creation—a cage with an intricate latch that an animal couldn't open. It was also built into a wagon, so that his men wouldn't have to lift the animals. There was a ramp that they could use to guide the animals and shut them in without injury.

Tyler had been proud of the design when he came up with it as a child, showing it to his father. His father had burst with pride as he looked at it, never knowing that it would one day be used to hold monsters.

Each of the men climbed onto their wagons and drove their horses. Ordinary horses would die of fright if they were tied too long near a wolfkin. They often recognized wolfkin by smell, even if he was in human form. Howlers seemed to fall into that category even though they were neither wolfkin nor human.

Wraith horses, on the other hand, could take on a wolfkin in a fight and often win. Tyler didn't know if they were natural enemies, or if the unnatural situation of being enslaved had them all at each other's throats. He supposed he'd never know.

He wished he could take the wraith horses on hunts with him. It wasn't the flaming mane and tail that was the problem. The forest hardly ever caught on fire, and when it did, it never grew large. The forest took care of itself.

The problem was the wolfkin. Regardless of which direction the wind was blowing, wolfkin seemed to sense wraith horses. He might as well wear bells all over himself and yell into the woods that he was hunting.

To keep the wraith horses from kicking the metal cages into bits, they only used horses that were exhausted. It was such a waste of the magnificent creatures to have them pull a wagon, but they were the only ones who could do it. The only other option was to use the king's slaves, and Tyler wouldn't do that unless ordered to.

Two of the wraith horses were little more than sagging hide over bones. The hide was torn and flapping in places, showing the bone and sinew beneath it. Their manes and tails burned bright, though.

The horse pulling the girl's cage was muscular and burned the brightest. The flames were crimson and yellow, dancing along the horse's neck and swinging along the tail as the wraith horse moved. It felt fitting that the girl had the strongest and brightest horse.

Tyler watched as the girl's wagon split off from the rest. He followed, walking at a comfortable pace—not so fast as to betray his eagerness; not so slow as to bring suspicion. He wanted to make sure that she was settled with proper food and water. He wanted her to be able to get a decent night's sleep and recover.

Because tomorrow, he would start her training.

CHAPTER 6

*R*uby woke up with so many aches and pains that she groaned even before knowing if it was safe to make a sound. Her eyes flew open as soon as she realized that she'd made noise in a dangerous place.

What she saw didn't feel dangerous at all. That by itself was suspicious.

Sunlight hurt her eyes, and she had to shut them again as soon as she opened them. She was left with a black-and-white impression of a barn with the doors wide open and letting the sun stream through. She thought she saw cows and sheep—some chickens, maybe.

She opened her eyes slowly this time, letting her long lashes filter the light until her eyes adjusted. She really was in a barn that was drenched with sunlight. The cows chewed on their hay and the chickens clucked by the open doors.

Ruby lay on a pile of fresh hay at the far end of the barn. She tried to make sense of what she was seeing.

When was the last time she'd slept in on a sunny day? Sometime during the week before she was taken for the Midnight Hunt, perhaps.

Since then, she had rarely seen the sun at all except from the inside of a crowded pen of slaves and prisoners. Ruby hadn't known until then that the hunters sometimes captured victims during the hunt and kept them. Mostly, they were used to do the drudge work in the castle. But when the moon became full, everyone lived in fear of the guards who dragged away those who were unlucky enough to catch their attention.

She'd survived that, though, hadn't she? Last night had been the worst she could remember. She tried to blot out the thoughts of the Midnight dungeons and the monster she'd had to fight.

Ruby did her best to cloud the memories over with this morning's sunshine and the soft clucking of chickens. The chickens didn't sound afraid.

A tiny flame of hope lit in Ruby's heart.

Had Gran managed to rescue her?

As soon as the thought emerged, she buried it. Hope could be dangerous.

Still, the thought refused to go away. It had been years since she'd last seen her grandmother, but Gran was not the type to give up.

Ruby pushed herself off the hay, moving stiffly and painfully. All her muscles and joints screamed. How long had she been sleeping?

The sun looked bright in the way it only did midday. The days had been getting shorter recently, so it was easier to tell the time when it was day.

Beside her was a large plate of food. Thin wafers of bread, balls of cheese, pickled radishes, dried fish, and grapes. Next to the plate was a pitcher of red liquid. At first, she thought the pitcher was filled with blood, but as soon as she saw the effervescence, she knew it was just beet kvass.

Her stomach grumbled as soon as she saw the food. She

didn't even care if it was poisoned. It was a better way to die than all the other ways she'd experienced lately. She stuffed it into her mouth as fast as she could.

She had no idea what was happening or why she was here, but whatever the reason, she didn't want to let this chance pass. She couldn't remember the last time she'd had a decent meal.

And this meal was as good as the king's. The bread was airy, with just enough crunch to make it pleasurable to eat. It was sweet too, layered with honey. The entire meal was delicious, and every bite burst with flavor in her mouth.

As she ate, Ruby thought through the ways that she could have ended up here. She'd been at the castle for...how long? Two years? Three? Maybe even four. She'd never had anything close to this luxury.

She allowed herself to think about the possibility that she had been rescued by Gran or some of her old friends from her Wild War days. Gran's friends all had gray hair, if they had any hair left at all, but they were the fiercest group of people Ruby had ever known. They had been spies and assassins, guards and rangers during the wars. Only they could have rescued her out of the infamous dungeons of Midnight Castle.

Ruby trembled all over just thinking about the possibility. Could it be true?

Of course not.

But she couldn't help but be sucked into the fantasy.

They could have hidden her here to recover. They couldn't take her back to Gran's house because Ruby would be a fugitive. They'd have to hide her until the king's men forgot about her.

The more she thought about it, the more she got lost in the possibility. She tried to stay cautious and keep the hope manageable, but it had been so long since she'd felt hope that she couldn't bear to let it go.

By the time she was done eating, there wasn't a crumb left on the plate or a drop left in the pitcher. Gran's friends could have made the food. That was the great thing about them—they were all quite talented. Gran used to say that some of her friends could cook or kill with equal ease.

Ruby stood up and stretched her neck and shoulders. She performed light drills to test out her body. Every muscle ached enough to remind her just how close death had been last night. The old, familiar drills helped soothe both Ruby's worries and her muscles.

When she was ready, she walked through the barn. It was time to find out if she'd really been rescued and thank whoever had hidden her. She loathed leaving this haven, though. She liked feeling the hope that her ordeal was finally over. So she lingered.

On her way to the barn opening, she petted a fat cow who chewed her cud and lowed at her. She smiled at the fluffy sheep that was in another pen. They bleated as she neared, then came up to her. She knew they wanted a treat, but she didn't have any, so she petted them instead.

The chickens near the doorway scattered out of the way as she walked through them. Beyond the barn doorway was a normal barnyard with bales of hay and a pen in front of her.

Ruby stepped into the sunshine.

Sunshine.

How long had it been? As soon as the sun's warmth touched her skin, her muscles relaxed in a way that they hadn't for far too long.

She smiled up at the sky, even as tears pooled in her eyes. The warmth of the sun on her face was like hearing Gran's voice telling her that everything would be all right. Ruby opened her arms as if she could embrace the sun, soaking it in.

That was when she heard the growl.

Ruby froze, realizing how silly she'd been to let her guard down so completely.

$\mathcal{T}$yler watched the girl as she slept in the barn. He was still and silent among the shadows. This was no different than waiting for game in the forest. He'd done that all his life, still as a rock and watchful for hours.

Sunlight streamed in through the doorway and between the wooden slats that made up the wall. It was a rare day full of sunshine and warmth. The light caressed the girl's head, highlighting the fire in her hair.

When she woke, her lashes fluttered before unveiling her deep green eyes. He watched as she went from cautious confusion to a dawning hope.

Hope.

How long had it been since he'd seen someone be hopeful? He could see that she was trying to remain cautious, but her happiness was palpable.

Tyler frowned. This was unexpected.

It had been a long time since he'd seen happiness in its pure form. This wasn't the happiness of the royal court, where someone else's misfortune was involved. He was witnessing something fresh and honest.

He'd occasionally glimpsed happiness on the face of peasants and lower merchants, but never in its pure form. It was typically tinged with the knowledge that this moment of joy would pass onto a moment of misery, as was typical in the Kingdom of Midnight. But not this girl.

She ate every morsel on the plate, stuffing her mouth as quickly as she could. She ate the way people did when they were both starved and worried that someone would take the food away from them. He couldn't tell if she was genuinely worried in this moment or if it was just habit.

The girl looked around cautiously, looking longingly at the square of sunshine by the doorway. Then she did a curious thing. She began a routine of light drills. Soldiers and hunters sometimes went through similar drills when practicing their training.

That was at odds with the rest of her behavior. She had obviously done it countless times, smooth and with perfect form. Yet no soldier looked so innocent and hopeful, not with the horrors they regularly faced.

And she had faced a true horror last night, hadn't she? Was she daft? Or perhaps so injured that she'd lost her memory of the traumatic events? Sometimes, that happened after a terrifying event.

Then a frightening thought occurred to him. What if she was a wild fairy?

What he was seeing could be a glamour. It would explain the girl's lack of fright, her strength to kill a howler, and the happiness he saw in her. It would also explain how she was more alluring than any creature he'd ever seen.

He steeled his heart against her. A wild fairy could tear a man to pieces from the inside out. Men who had been found dead under the spell of a wild fairy had been found grinning with a look so happy that living men envied him.

A wild fairy was a dangerous creature. If he had one on his hands, Tyler was in deep trouble.

The girl walked to the animals in their pens. She moved with grace as though she was gliding underwater. Light on her feet, willowy and ethereal. That only jangled Tyler's nerves even more.

When she reached the animals, Tyler tensed. A wild fairy could easily devour the animals. He'd never actually seen one, but he'd heard old stories from the Wild Wars. Perhaps he was about to witness for himself how she'd survived the attack last night.

Instead of devouring the barn animals, though, she cooed at them and petted them. The animals nuzzled her. They probably would have died of fright if she were a wild fairy or a howler.

Tyler shook his head as he watched her. With the sunshine streaming in, she looked like she belonged in a children's painting from a bygone era when stories ended with "and they lived happily ever after."

No, she was no wild fairy. She was a mere girl, smiling at the animals like a child in a young woman's body.

The oddest sensation flowed through him as he watched her chat easily with the animals. There was kindness in her.

That wasn't something that Tyler had seen in years. He supposed that people were sometimes kind behind closed doors, but showing it in public just showed weakness to your enemies. And in Midnight, everyone had enemies.

How could this girl kill anything? She was no monster, no wild anything. From what he could see, she would be no threat to anyone other than someone who tracked mud into her house. He was sure she'd give that person a scolding, as would any other girl destined to be a house mother.

Tyler shook his head as he hid in the shadows. The final test would be Shadow.

Tyler watched carefully as the girl stepped outside the barn. He almost felt a niggling remorse as he watched her soak in the sunshine.

Then he heard Shadow growl.

The girl froze.

Now, he would see what she was truly made of.

CHAPTER 8

*A*n enormous black dog snarled at Ruby, watching her with intense eyes.

His muscles rippled through his shiny coat and saliva drooled down his fangs. His hackles were up, and his muzzle wrinkled dangerously.

This was one of the king's hunting dogs. She'd seen enough of them in the forest to recognize it. There wasn't a person in Midnight who wasn't terrified of the Dark King's dogs.

She took a step back, frantically scanning her surroundings for anything she could use to defend herself. All she saw were some empty barrels beside her.

As the Midnight dog ran toward her, she flipped the nearest barrel over herself.

She pushed herself back against the barn wall and braced against the rounded sides of the barrel. The dog slammed against the barrel.

She staggered sideways but managed to stay upright. If she let the dog flip the barrel, she'd be helpless and trapped with the dog at her feet.

The dog growled and clawed frantically at the wood, shoving his powerful body against it.

Ruby braced against the barn wall and the curved wood around her as firmly as she could, trying her best to keep the barrel in place.

A sharp whistle pierced the air.

The Midnight dog immediately quieted and stopped pushing.

Ruby continued to brace herself, trying to hear what was happening outside her barrel. The last thing she needed was to be taken off guard. One surprise shove, and that would be the end of her.

"You can come out now," said a man. He sounded disappointed.

She waited a breath or two, not sure if it was safe to come out.

"I said come out. Are you going to stay there all day?" Now, he sounded annoyed.

Ruby cautiously pushed up the edge of the barrel with her foot and waited to see what would happen. When the dog didn't attack, she shoved the barrel off as quickly as she could. The last thing she wanted was to be blind and halfway out of a barrel during an attack.

The hunter who had taken her out of the dungeon stood where the dog had first shown up. The dog was now sitting beside him.

All Midnight dogs were dangerous, just as all of the Dark King's men were dangerous. It did confuse her, though, to see the dog looking so…pleased.

Ruby couldn't understand what had happened. This man couldn't be her rescuer. Was this a raid? Had her grandmother's friends been arrested?

She didn't think so. This hunter was the last thing she

remembered before passing out. He could have been part of Gran's network, but Ruby doubted it.

He looked too young to be in charge, but the other men had taken his orders last night. Also, his boots and the carved hilt of the knife at his belt showed fine workmanship that indicated a high rank among the king's officials.

She wanted to hide under the barrel until he went away, but she knew from experience that there was no hiding from the king's twisted plans. The realization that she had not been rescued—and would never be rescued—was sinking in.

The hunter glared at her. "What did you expect to happen while you hid like a coward? Did you expect the dog to get bored and go away?"

"He did go away."

"Only because this was a test. In the real world, you'd be dead. Are you sure you killed that beast in your cell by yourself?"

Ruby wanted to close her eyes so she could try to blot out the violent memories. "Yes. I am a killer."

Would this hunter condemn her for it or admire her?

"And you did that with your bare hands? You, who hide under barrels and cower when I raise my voice?"

Ruby took a deep breath. She did cower when he raised his voice. It was habit from dealing with the castle guards. They didn't like it when they thought that a prisoner wasn't intimidated. If you cowered or seemed afraid, they ignored you. If you challenged them by looking right in their eyes, they made an example of you.

Ruby tried to think of flowers. Flowers were a luxury item for rich families, but to Ruby, they reminded her of her grandmother. Gran had a way with flowers.

It normally comforted Ruby to think of her grandmother's flower stand. She did it when she needed to blot out the bad thoughts. It helped her hold on to the person she was when they first brought her to Midnight Castle.

The worker pens had been crowded and full of vermin, but everyone slept in a tight group, especially during the full moon. Everyone believed that getting one of the coveted spots in the center of the huddle was the ticket to survival. Ruby was one of the few who knew better.

The guards came at every full moon to pick out people and drag them away into the night. Hardly anyone ever came back. And those few who did never spoke about what happened to them during the night.

Some were lucky and were never chosen. Some were clever and made deals with the guards to ensure they weren't selected, at least for that full moon.

Those few who were dragged away but managed to return the next morning were never the same again. Their hands shook and they had a hard time with their labors in the upcoming weeks.

And then there was Ruby. She had been selected many times. It hadn't mattered whether she'd slept in the center of the huddle or the outside.

She was certain that she'd been picked randomly the first couple of times, but after that, the guards began to take bets on whether she'd make it back the next morning. She guessed that even the guards didn't know what happened to the people they chose.

Ruby breathed deep to blot out the memories and thought about Gran's flowers. Tried to smell the scent of her summer garden.

She had to strain to do it, because it was getting harder to remember what that was like.

CHAPTER 9

*T*he girl was insisting that she killed the howler with her bare hands. Tyler couldn't fathom why she would not tell him what truly happened in that cell.

"Are you a braggart?" he asked. "Does it please you to claim that you did a courageous and miraculous thing?"

Many soldiers and workers were braggarts. Tyler was used to men's exaggerations. But he'd never seen a slip of a girl like this one make up such stories, especially when it came to killing monsters.

"I would never." She looked contrite.

Tyler was used to liars. The court was full of them, and they'd honed his skepticism early in life. He didn't think she was lying, though.

"Then how can a dandelion like you who runs from a friendly dog kill a howler?"

"He's not friendly." She sounded indignant. This was the first time he'd heard any fire in her. "He almost killed me."

"Did you hear that, Shadow? You're a killer."

Right on time, Shadow snarled low and menacing. His training was coming along well.

Whatever she wanted to say, the growl convinced her to keep quiet. She was a careful one. She knew when to hold her tongue.

That would be good in court and among people, but that kind of polite restraint would be useless on a hunt. Whatever had happened in that cell, he couldn't reconcile it with this girl. From everything he'd seen, she was a gentle soul.

Gentle souls got torn to shreds in Midnight. So how was she still alive?

"What happened that night in the cell?" He crossed his arms. "Your life depends on telling me the truth."

"I..." Her voice trembled. "He...it...attacked me."

"And?"

"And I defended myself. Why did you make your 'friendly' dog attack me?"

"Because I wanted to see how you handle an attack. How did you defend yourself against the howler? Did you hide under a barrel?"

"If only the guards had had the decency to provide one in the dungeons."

"What did you do to defend yourself then?"

"I broke his finger." Her voice came out low, as if she wished she hadn't had to do it.

"Then what?"

She shook her head. "It was all a blur. I don't really remember."

"You broke his finger? And then did you ask him nicely to die? Were you so sweet and good that he broke his own back and neck rather than eat you? Is that what happened?"

She bowed her head.

Tyler frowned. Anyone with enough fire in her to kill a howler would be yelling back at him by now. But this girl wasn't even arguing. Anyone else would have been crowing about how he'd slain an enormous, twisted monster with his bare hands, embellishing every part of the fight.

This girl didn't look at all proud of her kill. If anything, she looked ashamed of it.

"What would you do if I set my dog on you right now? If I commanded him to tear your throat out, would you let him?"

She looked cautiously at Shadow. "You said he was friendly."

"Right up to the moment when I give the kill command."

She took a deep breath and let it out slowly. "Then do it. I'm ready. Just please don't punish anyone else for my deeds."

She closed her eyes and stood there like a martyr, obviously trying to look serene. But the trembling gave her away. A part of her might be trying to give up, but the rest of her still wanted to live.

Tyler sighed. What was he supposed to do with her? He shook his head, mocking himself for being so foolish. How could he have thought for a moment that she was a killer?

"Tell me what really happened in the dungeon, and I'll let you go home."

Her eyes opened slowly. It was hard to see hope there. She was naive and still thought there was a chance for happiness in the world. He felt a twinge in his chest over that. It was so unexpected and subtle that he was surprised he even recognized that small twinge of guilt.

"Home?" She swallowed. "You'll really let me go home?"

"Tell me what really happened. Did a guard kill the howler?"

"I killed him."

Then she told him the details of what happened. How the howler attacked and trapped her with his thick arms. How she'd broken his little finger before he could bite into her. How she gouged his eyes, then snapped his knee.

Despite her earlier claim of not remembering, her recall

was remarkable. It was as though she'd been trained in the art of military reporting. She knew the dimensions of her cell, the size and approximate weight of her enemy, the level of light streaming in through the moon roof.

She hadn't known that the beast would continue to come after her after she'd injured him so much. Tyler guessed that she didn't want to kill the beast, even though it clearly would have killed her.

Eventually, she did what she needed to. She managed to fend off the howler until she got behind him and snapped his neck. It would take impressive agility and strength for someone to do that.

Tyler grilled her on her techniques. How could a girl with her relative lack of strength snap the neck of such a creature? It was impossible.

He made her demonstrate, forcing her to relive the fight.

He watched her carefully as she mimed the encounter. He had been mistaken earlier when he watched her in the barn. She moved with grace all right, but it wasn't light and ethereal as he had thought. Her body moved with the grace of a predator. She moved like a street fighter who'd been trained from birth.

Tyler couldn't help but grin. He couldn't believe his luck.

He'd found the bait he'd been looking for.

CHAPTER 10

"Who is your grandmother?" asked the hunter. "She's the one who trained you—isn't that what you said last night?"

Warning bells went off in Ruby's head. No one betrayed the identity of anyone else in her grandmother's circle. It had been a long-ingrained habit of the old wars that Ruby had learned at an early age. She must have been almost delirious with exhaustion last night when she spoke of her grandmother.

The hunter looked pleased. Earlier, he'd seemed disappointed with Ruby, looking almost eager to dismiss her. But once she began showing him how she'd killed the beast that attacked her, a spark of wonder came into his eyes. Even now, he was grinning.

"Why? My grandmother is no one of any importance."

"She trained you well, even as a child. Just imagine how well she could train my own men."

"She doesn't do that anymore, not with her swollen joints. She's quite old and frail. She's lucky to be able to get out of bed on a good day."

Gran would laugh if she heard Ruby. That woman could be blindfolded and still beat a Dark King's soldier in a fight.

"May I go home now?"

The hunter's grin dried up.

"You said I could go home if I told you what happened. I told you every detail. It's your turn to fulfill your part of the bargain."

Ruby's heart hammered. She knew that many people would cheat if they could. But she'd had no choice but to appeal to this man's decency. He had all the power here.

"I lied," he said. He said it with confidence, knowing that there was nothing she could do about it. "Now that I know that you really are capable of killing a beast, I have need of your services."

"Why would I serve someone who lies to me?"

"Everyone lies. But if you prefer, I'll tell you the truth from now on."

"You're teaching me to think of you as saying nothing but lies. So how can I believe you?"

"Good. Your kin may have taught you to fight, but your education is sorely lacking in people. Now that you're here in court, know that everyone is a liar. Everyone will kill you without a second thought if it gains them a coin or an advantage. From now on, I am the only one you can trust."

Ruby threw him a skeptical look.

"I see that you're a fast learner. I like that. You'll learn to trust that I will reward loyalty and punish disobedience. We don't have a lot of time, so you'll need to learn fast."

"Time until what?"

Ruby didn't like the impulse to address him as "my lord." She'd done it all the time when she helped her grandmother sell flowers at her stall. The nobles expected it and the wealthy merchants enjoyed it. But even though flattery would be the clever thing to do here, she wouldn't let herself address him that way.

"Time until the next full moon. We'll be going on your first hunt as soon as possible."

Ruby's stomach churned. The thought of having to go into the forest on the full moon made her want to vomit.

Her breath came out ragged, and she could feel the blood draining from her face. The Dark King's hunt was what had brought her here in the first place.

The hunter watched her carefully. She was sure he saw every emotion that crossed her mind.

"Are you afraid?" he asked.

"Of course. Everyone is afraid of the hunts."

"Not the hunters."

She scoffed. In that one sound she let every bit of her disgust show. "That's right, the *brave* hunters who capture helpless girls like me and toss them into dungeons to be eaten by beasts."

He arched a brow. "So you do have opinions."

"Everyone has an opinion on the hunts."

"Very few know of this particular hunt."

Ruby watched him carefully. Was he toying with her? Everyone knew about the Midnight Hunts. "What do you mean?"

"This is the true hunt, not the one that's put on for the public for show. That hunt is a circus, meant to keep eyes and questions away from other events."

Ruby shook her head. The Midnight Hunt that took place on the full moon was infamous in its cruelty and body count. How could there be another hunt that no one knew about?

"I would rather die than be part of another hunt." Ruby's hands curled into fists, but she couldn't keep them from trembling.

He watched her with not an ounce of compassion in his

eyes. "A hunter who shows fear will quickly become dead meat."

"What does that have to do with me?"

"You're no good to me dead."

Ruby blinked in confusion. All she could do was stare at him, trying to make sense of what he was saying.

He sighed, as though tired of the conversation. "At this rate, you'll be the worst hunter on my team."

"Hunter?" Had she heard him right? He intended for her to be one of his hunters and not the prey?

"We'd better start your training as soon as possible. We don't have much time to shape you into something worth bringing into the forest on a full moon."

"What kind of training?" Did he want to teach her how to ride a horse through the woods? To understand the signals that hunters used?

He turned away, making it clear he was done with the conversation. His dog turned with him, ever attentive to his master.

"Shadow," he said casually as he pointed to Ruby. "Attack."

The Midnight dog instantly turned and ran at Ruby.

CHAPTER 11

The girl survived everything Tyler threw at her. At least, that was what his men reported to him. He hadn't gone back to her since the first day when he watched her wake in the barn. He'd been busy overseeing his plans for the hunts.

The wild wolfkin were growing in numbers, and he'd heard rumors that some men were even going into the forest to volunteer themselves to the beasts. Had the kingdom become so twisted as to make sacrificing yourself a better choice than living as a man?

He'd meant to check in on the girl sooner, but being a huntsman in these dark times demanded everything from him. He hardly had time to sleep and eat.

Yet it hadn't stopped him from asking questions about her. He wasn't surprised to learn that she was from the laborer's pool. That was where many of the kingdom's criminals and captives from the royal hunts ended up. That was also where many of the victims for the king's howlers came from.

Tyler knew only a little about what happened with the

howlers before they ended up in the dungeons. He knew there was a process that involved dark magic and that victims were used as part of the monster whelp training.

He'd heard that they trained the whelps by teaching them to attack weak people tied up in bags. The monster whelps were meant to grow into wolfkin, but the howlers were the closest that the king's sorcerers had managed. Rumor had it that the whelps created by dark magic were a collection of the most unnatural creatures.

Tyler was surprised to learn that the girl who'd survived the night in the dungeon had been tossed to the whelps multiple times. He'd thought that those victims rarely survived. How could they even fight while tied in a bag?

It must be exaggerated gossip.

How long had it been since he'd started her training? It was harder to tell now that there were three moons in the sky, but he knew it had been weeks.

He should have put her out there on the last hunt. But she wouldn't have survived. She had the raw skills, but her confidence had not caught up to her abilities.

Of all the bait he'd found, she was the most interesting, and he was loath to lose her on the first run. She needed seasoning to have a chance at survival out in the woods. If she'd had confidence in her abilities to begin with, she might never have been caught in the first place.

Tyler had to admit that he felt an odd reluctance to see her again.

He'd felt like that before with animals that he knew were slated for slaughter. It was better not to get attached. He'd learned at an early age not to name the slaughter animals, not to look too closely at their eyes, not to spend too much time with them. He thought he'd outgrown that kind of sentimentality, but he was surprised to find that perhaps he hadn't.

When Tyler finally went to check on the girl, he was expecting that she would either be broken or bitter. She was neither.

He watched the training from the roof of one of the buildings around the corral. From here, he had a clear view of the barn.

He'd kept the girl in the barn since it seemed like the safest place for her. The howlers were far enough away that they wouldn't catch her scent, and the men who worked here were gentler than the ones who worked the monster yard. Tyler would probably pay for his soft-heartedness in the end, since it wouldn't do the girl any favors to coddle her.

He had thought that he might not see her again until her first hunt. If she survived, he'd consider working with her directly. But the chances of that happening were so slim as to be almost laughable.

The reports he'd been getting from his trainers were surprising, though, and he had to come see for himself. It turned out that the girl knew how to use weapons. She seemed to be particularly good with the bow and knife, but she was passable with almost any weapon they put into her hands.

It would take years for a person to become proficient with weapons. Just how long had she been training? Whoever her grandmother was, she must have thought the Wild Wars would start again sometime during her granddaughter's life. Many of that generation thought so, especially the old soldiers and spies. They were convinced that the old wars had never actually ended, despite the fact that the Dark King had ascended the throne by winning the war the year Tyler was born.

Tyler stood on the roof and waited. The sun warmed his skin and hair. Hadn't it been sunny the last time he'd seen her too? It was ridiculous to associate this girl with the warmth of the sun, but there was a part of him that did.

His men opened the barn door.

The girl stood there with watchful eyes. The slope of her shoulders looked resigned rather than tensing for action. That was not a good sign. Perhaps his men were smitten with her and had exaggerated their reports.

A breeze caught her hair and teased it away from her face. Red and gold highlights played on her locks, shifting with the breeze. Instead of the filthy dress he'd seen on her the last time, she now wore the clothes of a hunter. Hard leather boots went up to her thighs. A fitted leather tunic clung to her body, protecting both her front and back. Her arms were also covered in hard leather, leaving only her elbows bare.

The usual leather armor was too heavy for the girl, so they'd had to make a special tunic just for her. Heavy enough to resist sharp fangs, yet light and flexible enough for her to run and fight in.

She looked like a warrior of old, walking straight out of one of the castle tapestries. The only thing that set her apart was that her hair was unbraided. He'd sent orders for her to keep her hair down. He didn't want to her to look like a warrior, even if he wanted her to fight like one.

Her hair would attract attention. It promised all kinds of feminine secrets to both beasts and men alike.

He'd have to hide her armor and weapons, but that was a simple matter of having a large enough cloak to cover her in. He wanted her noticeable, though, as all bait needed to be. A brightly colored cloak would do the trick. Perhaps red?

Yes. A blood-red cloak would be perfect.

The girl stood alone in the barn doorway as Tyler's men disappeared into the shadows. The barn animals began to low and bleat in a cacophony of rising panic. Tyler instinctively gripped the hilt of his knife strapped to his thigh.

For a moment, nothing moved in the yard except for the girl's hair.

Then came the sound of cages opening.

Tyler watched the girl as the Midnight dogs were released somewhere beyond where he could see. She tensed, scanning the yard. She smoothly pulled out knives from her boots, holding one in each hand as she began moving.

Good. She was choosing her own place to fight rather than staying where she was. If she stayed by the doors, she'd be trapped in the barn. Under normal conditions, there would be advantages there, but his men had made sure that none of those were available to her.

The growls grew and got closer. Long shadows reached out from below Tyler's building.

The shadows were too long, too upright. These weren't Midnight dogs approaching the girl. These were full-grown howlers.

CHAPTER 12

This time, Ruby counted three. One from the left, one from the right, and one coming at her from the front. The trainers had separated the beasts so that she was almost surrounded.

She moved toward the one to her right. He sounded the closest.

Before the barn doors opened, her instincts had been to pretend that she was sick. But that ploy only ever worked on her father. These trainers were harder than her grandmother, so it was merely a sign of Ruby's desperation that she wanted to resort to her earliest avoidance tactics. She wasn't a baby anymore, and even if she was, these men wouldn't care.

Now that she was faced with life or death, all thoughts of avoidance disappeared. The trainers toyed with her. They'd said she'd fight one. Instead, they released three howlers all at once.

Her only chance was to fight them one at a time. With her heart pounding in her throat, she moved as quickly as she could to the first beast.

He was a giant. Part wolf, part man. Like the other howlers she'd seen, he hadn't—or couldn't—fully turn.

Neither beast nor wolf, he had hair all over his muscular limbs and shoulders. His snout was elongated to accommodate all those sharp teeth. His hands and feet were more paw-like, although not quite fingerless. He moved sometimes on two limbs and sometimes on four, as if he couldn't figure out which felt more natural. Like everything at Midnight Castle, he was a twisted bastardization that could mimic neither man nor wolfkin.

When he came out of the shadows, he came right for her.

Ruby was ready. She whistled loudly as she slashed with her blades.

The howler must have remembered some of what it was like to be a man. He dodged the blades.

But he couldn't dodge Shadow.

The Midnight Dog practically flew onto the howler, fearless and full of fury. He was a ball of muscle and a great distraction.

Ruby sliced through the wolfkin's throat before he could sink his teeth into Shadow.

The dog, now slick with blood, turned with her toward the other howler. Two of them came at her from different directions. She couldn't think of a way to separate them long enough for her to fight only one.

So she reached into her pocket and tossed the meat she'd stowed. For several meals, she'd wrapped the meat from her plate and hidden it away, defending it against rats. Not every weapon had to be forged from metal.

The howler to her right automatically caught the meat in his mouth. That gave her a moment to move and put the remaining monster between her and the other beast.

Shadow played their game of distraction—moving in and out toward the monster. The dog was great at this. Ruby didn't like risking him, but she had no choice but to work with what she had.

She cut the monster in fast strokes. It was hard to kill a howler unless she managed to stab in just the right places, but it was easy to slice them enough to bleed.

The last howler was just as twisted and unnatural as she'd guessed. He couldn't resist the blood. It attacked the wounded howler, knowing that it was easier prey than she.

Ruby wanted to look away from the carnage as monster attacked monster. But she knew better than to turn her back on an enemy. Instead, she slowly backed away, bringing Shadow with her.

When it was over, the trainers captured the remaining howler and dragged him back to his cage. The bloody beast howled into the air, beating its chest as if it thought it was an ape.

Ruby shook her head as she watched the men drag the abomination away. She bent down to pet Shadow and wiped the blood from his eyes.

Footsteps approached, crunching gravel.

Shadow barked a greeting and trotted over to the man. He was the hunter who'd taken her out of the dungeon. He looked lordly and clean compared to her trainers. His leather was well oiled, his dark hair freshly washed and gleaming in the light. He had none of the greasiness or griminess of her trainers.

She'd heard the trainers talk about him. They called him the Huntsman. She'd pieced together that he was in charge of this operation, and that the men took orders from him. The trainers were also hunters, but compared to the Huntsman, they were a different breed.

She thought that maybe he might be pleased with her progress—the trainers had certainly been. They weren't the type to praise, but she could see by their faces that she'd surpassed anything they'd expected. Today, she'd outperformed everything she'd done before. Not only had she fought off a howler—she'd won against three.

Rather than being impressed, though, the Huntsman glared at her. He looked down at Shadow with a frown, giving him a disapproving look.

Shadow seemed oblivious and lolled his tongue, panting. When he looked like that, he looked like he was grinning. That always charmed Ruby, but it just seemed to annoy the Huntsman.

"Who assigned my dog to you?" he demanded.

"Nobody," said Ruby. "We just became friends."

"My dogs do not have friends. They are hunting animals, trained for a specific job. He was supposed to terrorize you, not lick your face." He said that to Shadow, who just grinned at him.

"He did terrorize me. For days."

"And? Did one of my men get sweet on you and order Shadow to be friendly?" He looked ready to throttle whoever had done that.

"No. I saved my food and shared it with him."

He thought about that for a moment. "You wield your food like a weapon."

"Everything can be a weapon." It was a familiar saying of her grandmother's.

"So you bribed my dog."

"I just fought off three howlers, and all you can do is complain about your dog being my friend?"

"I have far more to complain about. The men will hear from me."

"And what is it that you didn't like?"

"First, you won't have dogs at your beck and call when we're out in the woods. Second, these howlers are broken and domesticated. They're not even fully turned into domesticated wolfkin, much less a wild one. You won't be able to bribe or distract a wild wolfkin with a piece of pork."

Ruby had been feeling great about the fight until now. "You don't think I did well?"

He pointed toward the woods. "Out there, you would have died if you fought like that."

Her shoulders deflated. She'd worked so hard to figure out how to fight off the ever-increasing threats that the trainers had thrown at her. But deep inside, she'd known that these controlled fights would only take her so far.

She was going to die out there.

CHAPTER 13

yler was angrier with Shadow than with the girl. The more he saw her confidence crumble, the angrier he got at Shadow.

How could the dog betray Tyler like that? Hadn't he saved him as a puppy when it was clear that Shadow couldn't fend off the other dogs at feeding time? Runts like him usually got used as training bait for the more aggressive pups.

In a moment of weakness, Tyler had saved him to be his personal pet. His father had been taken away by the king's soldiers and had been missing for days, so the other hunters didn't look down on Tyler for taking on a pet as a distraction. Still, showing that kind of softness would only be allowed so many times before the other men took notice.

Shadow just grinned at him with his tongue lolling. He didn't have an ounce of remorse for the embarrassment he'd caused Tyler. What did his men think of Shadow's betrayal?

Then there was the girl.

He had to admit that perhaps his anger wasn't entirely anger. Deep down inside, he acknowledged that it was possible that he was just shaken up over what he'd witnessed.

The girl had fought like a demon. She'd fought not one, not two, but three howlers.

Those beasts were twisted and wrong, the way so many things were at Midnight Castle. They were as savage as any creature in the civilized lands.

Tyler could see the girl's confidence, and how impressed his men were at her fighting skills. She was clever and quick, agile and deadly. All of which was great.

He had been praying for someone like her for years. So why was he angry?

Because this girl was going to die.

She was going to be wasted on a hunt and never fully develop into the great hunter he knew she could be.

In the wild, the wolfkin turned all the way into the bodies of giant wolves. The Dark King's howlers were less than runts compared to them. They had some true wolfkin in captivity that turned all the way as well. But the king's wolfkin had been born in captivity and were never as fierce or deadly as the ones in the wild.

The girl's shoulders sank when he told her that her fighting tactics wouldn't work out in the wild. That they were fools to think that it would all translate into a fight for her life in a real attack.

He was glad that she understood the seriousness of the situation. Nothing could kill a hunter faster than overconfidence.

It was really Tyler's fault for not closely overseeing her training. His reluctance to get attached to a good piece of bait had landed him here.

The trainers would get an earful later. Tyler had to admit, though, that despite letting her think she was fighting the real thing, they'd done a great job with what they had.

Tyler would have been furious if they'd used a true wolfkin on her. They had a few that they'd caught in hunts, but they never lived long in captivity. They were truly wild and would be the closest thing to what she'd face out there, but they would have killed her, even with his men ready to stop the fight. The wild wolfkin were as unpredictable as they were fierce.

Tyler sighed. His anger and blame had come full circle.

It was unlike him to throw blame at everything and everyone. Perhaps he had been right to keep his distance from this girl. She had a way of turning his emotions into chaos.

"So my next fight will be with a real wolfkin?" the girl asked as though she thought she might have a chance to survive if she was very good.

Tyler thought about her question. She had the infuriating habit of constantly reminding him of her innocence.

The girl was more ready than any other bait he'd ever used. He couldn't justify her long training period. Lives were being lost every month over his reluctance to use her for bait. It was time.

"You'll be fighting real wolfkin in three days. There will be no trainers ready to save you. No friendly dogs to help you fight. No easy meat to distract the beasts. Do you understand?"

She nodded. She looked scared. That should have satisfied him, but instead, it made him feel worse. Was there no comfortable situation to be found around this girl?

"If you survive, I'll personally oversee your training."

He paused, seeing the resolve on her face. It was clear that she did not see his personal training as a reward.

"If you don't survive, I'll send word to your grandmother that you fought well."

She blinked twice, looking like she'd been punched in the gut. Her eyes began to shimmer with a sheen of tears.

Tears.

What kind of fighter was she?

He turned and walked away from her. He had no time to deal with a simpering milkmaid. A few steps in, he realized that Shadow was not by his side.

"Shadow," he growled.

The dog trotted up to him. Shadow didn't even have the decency to look ashamed. He even looked back at the girl.

"Traitor," Tyler mumbled.

Shadow whined.

"You never fought for me like that. Seems all you needed was a pretty face and a soft voice. Should I throw you in with your brothers and sisters to fend for yourself? Are you a fierce killer now?"

Shadow lolled his tongue out at him and grinned.

Tyler shook his head. He was approaching his men. They stood in a group with their heads down. They knew they were going to get a full rundown of everything that went wrong.

"Did you see?" asked Mathewson. "She's ready."

"She'll never be ready, not with the way you've been coddling her." He knew that was unfair, but he didn't care. It felt good to let his frustration out.

"But…" Mathewson frowned.

"But she's alive, yes."

It really wasn't their fault. He should have overseen her training personally. Besides, would he have done better? No amount of training could guarantee her safety once the hunt began.

"Let's try to keep her that way," said Tyler. "We have three days to prepare. We'll run through the scenario until then. I'll be attending."

His men nodded with a mix of fear and excitement. They weren't that different from the Midnight dogs—they all lived for the hunt.

CHAPTER 14

*I*n the next three days, everything changed for Ruby.

She'd gotten used to fighting in the barnyard. Little by little, the attacks had gone from one dog to several, then from one howler whelp to three grown monsters.

She'd survived it all. She'd even seen the growing respect of the trainers. They hadn't exactly befriended her, but they no longer treated her like a cur.

They didn't stop her when they saw that she was slowly making friends with Shadow. They even told her his name when she asked. They weren't a chatty bunch, at least not around her, but they did occasionally speak to her.

But after the Huntsman came to watch her fight, they stopped talking to her. Even when she asked a direct question, they stayed quiet and wouldn't meet her eyes. She wondered if farmers did that with their prized pigs before taking them to slaughter.

For three days, they took her into the woods. This wasn't the deep, dark forest of the hunts, but it was the edges of it.

They stayed along the border where they could easily see the open fields and get out fast if they needed to.

Ruby trembled all over when they took her into the cool, dim woods. Nothing good ever happened there. She'd grown up with horror stories of wild fairies and the twisted animals that lived there.

They said that once upon a time, this forest used to be a happy place. Those were the days of sunshine and roses, the times before the Wild Wars.

For as long as Ruby could remember, the forest had been the most dangerous and twisted place in all of Midnight. The only exception was the court where the Dark King reigned.

On the first day, they took her into the woods at dawn. They brought three wagons with them, a dozen hunters and several assistants. The Huntsman was there, leading the group.

They discussed where to position the wagons and which spots to place the hunters. They unpacked gear and weapons, discussed options and paced out locations.

Ruby stood among them, seemingly forgotten. She was all right with that. She needed to get her bearings and try to understand what was happening.

They were setting up for a trap. The wagons were stationed far enough away that it wouldn't be noticeable. The men were stationed both high and low, hiding so well that Ruby couldn't see them even though she knew where they were.

Ruby stood by a tree, trying to stay out of the way. She watched everyone carefully, especially the Huntsman. She was as still as the tree she leaned on, making sure that she didn't draw any attention.

This was the first time she'd been taken out of the barnyard. The barn had been a luxurious jail, but a jail nonetheless. They let her out when they wanted her to fight or when she was being closely watched. Here, she was surrounded by armed hunters, but as far as she could tell, no one was specifically assigned to watch her. They behaved as though they'd forgotten she was a prisoner.

She couldn't escape—there were too many of them. But the mere possibility of being set loose in an uncontrolled environment, one with no bars or locked doors, was so exciting that it made her tremble.

She tamped it down, careful not to show anything but curiosity. The men were afraid of these woods. She could sense it on their faces, their careful motions, their voices.

Ruby was no fool. She was afraid too, more than they were. But if she were to run into the woods, would they follow? What if she slipped away quietly while everyone was busy?

Everyone knew that this forest had a way of swallowing people. The villagers said that once you went in, you'd be lost forever. But Ruby knew that wasn't quite true.

The hunters went in every full moon. The woodcutters also went in and came back out. Her grandmother even had a hiding place there where she rescued victims of the hunt. Ruby probably wasn't supposed to know about that, but she did.

Could she find her way through the forest to her grandmother's house?

Ruby couldn't think of anyone else who would know what to do with her once she showed up at their door. Gran and her friends from the old wars had hidden lots of people for all kinds of reasons. Ruby had only heard the old war stories, but Gran had too many secrets and quiet conversations for Ruby to think that all of that underground work was done.

"Girl," said the Huntsman.

Ruby's attention flew to him. Had he been watching her while she'd been thinking about escape?

"Her name is—" began Mathewson, one of her trainers.

"Don't care," said the Huntsman. "I might bother to learn it if she survives the hunt. Until then, she has no name."

The Huntsman pointed at Ruby. "You. Come here."

She timidly walked over to him, unsure what he wanted with her.

He pulled a bundle of red cloth out of one of the sacks lying on the ground. He tossed it at her.

"Wear this. Make sure it doesn't drag or get in the way when you fight. If it does, tell me and I'll have the seamstress change it."

Ruby held the cloth up and saw that it was a hooded cloak. It was wool dyed blood red. When she wrapped it around her shoulders, the chill of the forest instantly disappeared.

She felt like a beacon in it, though. She'd never be able to move without being seen in this cloak.

"I can't hunt in this," she said.

"Leave that to us." The Huntsman looked at her appraisingly, scanning the edges of the cloak and the brightness of the color.

Why had they trained her to hunt if she was just going to stand around in a bright cloak while they did the hunting?

A terrible thought dawned on her.

"What will I be doing?" She knew the answer, but hoped he'd say something else.

"You'll be the bait. The wolfkin won't be able to resist when they see you."

Until now, Ruby hadn't been sure what to make of the Huntsman. Tall and handsome, clean and commanding—she'd wondered what kind of man he was beneath his hard exterior.

Shadow seemed to like him. And he had been the one to release her from the infamous dungeons beneath Midnight Castle. Even though she'd had to fight for her life every day since, she would have been long dead already if it hadn't been for him.

But now, she knew exactly how she felt about him. She hated the Huntsman.

CHAPTER 15

*O*n the first day, the group decided on the setup and location of everyone and every piece of equipment. Ruby's job seemed to be just to walk down the path over and over again while the hunters set up.

Of course, once they were done setting up, Ruby had to fight.

Luckily, this was a mock-up of a fight. The assistants pretended to be monsters and attacked Ruby as slowly as they could. While they fought in slow motion, the Huntsman orchestrated his men. He told them when and where to shoot, what his signals would be, when to jump out into the open.

The mock fight was not frightening, but it was exhausting. Ruby didn't realize how tiring it could be to hold an unbalanced position over and over again. She felt like an actress practicing a play for Market Day.

All the while, she looked for opportunities to escape, but found none. There were too many watching her.

When the sun began to set midafternoon, they packed up

and left the woods. Back in the barnyard, they set up and practiced well into the night.

On the second day, they repeated the same thing, but stayed in the woods through dusk. Then they practiced by moonlight in the barnyard.

On the third day, they stayed in the forest until well after dark. For hours, they practiced by the filtered light of the moon.

The moon was almost full, and after a few hours, the two crescent moons followed, adding even more light. In the barnyard, it had been bright enough to create moon shadows. But in the forest, everything was eerily dim. It was just enough to see, but the underbrush and trees took on a menacing darkness in the moonlight.

On the fourth day, they let Ruby sleep in late.

They gave her especially large meals, as they had done the last three days. Rather than a single plate, she woke up to three. They were piled with meats and vegetables, fruits and sweet cakes.

On the previous days, she'd eaten it all. But even as she stuffed herself, she worried that this was too generous. Were they fattening her up?

Not that the thought had stopped her from eating. She needed as much strength as she could get if she was going to survive the upcoming hunt.

But today, she found that she could barely finish one plate. She picked at her food both at breakfast and the midday meal. Rather than go at dawn, they allowed her a leisurely morning and early afternoon.

She spent that time practicing her defensive moves. She couldn't use weapons because they always took those away after her fights. So she practiced with sticks and her bow, even though she had no arrows.

The Huntsman came by while she was practicing.

"You should be resting," he said. "You have a long night ahead of you."

Ruby didn't reply. It wouldn't matter what she said. She was a prisoner. And until she could free herself, her opinions didn't matter.

"Come with me," he said. "I want to show you something."

She followed. She had decided that she hated him—yet her life depended on him. He was the only thing keeping her alive. If she couldn't escape, her only hope of staying alive was to be useful to him.

She followed him out of the barnyard. She'd never been allowed out of this area. Ruby memorized the path and watched carefully. Knowing the geography of the grounds might help her one day.

They walked through a row of cages that held the howlers. They looked not quite human but not quite wolfkin, either. They had arms and legs like a person, although they were particularly hairy and muscular. Their eyes were sunken and their noses and lips protruded into snouts. They had lips that split and bled, stretching but still unable to close over the sharp teeth that bulged out of their mouths.

Then she and the Huntsman walked into a different area. This was a large yard full of empty cages. Looking at how clean the cages were, Ruby guessed that they'd never been occupied.

The Huntsman walked over to the only cage that was occupied and stopped. This must be what he wanted to show her.

Inside the cage was a huge wolf. It was nothing like what she'd imagined. She thought that a wolf would be like the ones she'd seen in tapestries and drawings at the market— majestic and howling at the full moon. She'd been secretly attracted to their wild spirit and beauty.

Of course, a wolf was not the same as a wolfkin. She'd

always known that, yet she still assumed that a wolfkin would look just like the wolves in those paintings.

But what she saw here struck instant fear into her. This creature looked like a giant wolf, except that he gave off the feeling that he was far more than a wolf. She was surprised by the direct stare. The calculating look behind his eyes.

He was assessing her.

She couldn't tell if the wolfkin wanted to eat her or figure out how to use her to get him out. Probably both. But she could tell that he was clever enough to use her first before eating her.

Then the creature's eyes moved to the Huntsman. She saw pure hatred and murder in the creature now. It showed in every part of the beast—his eyes, his pulled ears and lips, in the way he crouched and almost slithered around in his cage.

The fur wasn't what she'd expected, either. It was greasy and spiky, not at all the soft and majestic coat of the wolves in the tapestries and paintings. The wolfkin smelled of dark loam and urine.

Ruby didn't want to get close, but the Huntsman beckoned her to the cage.

"This is what you'll be dealing with out there tonight." The Huntsman gestured to the beast. "I wanted you to see one, so that you aren't taken off guard in the forest."

Ruby nodded. Her heart hammered and her breath came fast and shallow. This creature couldn't be fought. It was too big, too strong, too cunning.

"We've captured a few over the years. Not many." He pointed to another cage behind a stack of barrels. "We have another one over there."

Around the barrels, Ruby caught a glimpse of silver fur and sharp claws. The color of the beast's fur reminded Ruby of her grandmother's hair.

"Why do you have them separated?" she asked.

"She gets very aggressive whenever she sees this one being taken away. She's calmer when she can't see him at all."

The silver wolfkin howled in a long sound of mourning.

"They don't survive long in captivity," he said.

"What do you want with them?" Her voice came out breathless.

"That's the Dark King's business. All you need to know is that we need to capture as many as possible. The only problem is that these beasts would rather die than be enslaved."

"But I heard the Dark King already has wolfkin. They bring them out during the royal hunts."

"They're mostly an exotic prize that displays the king's powers. But they're so rare that even the royal family has to share them."

"So they don't all die in captivity?"

"The king's pets were born and raised in captivity. We managed to capture a couple of pregnant wolfkin. The mothers died soon after giving birth."

The wolfkin in the cage growled ferociously, as though angry at what he'd just heard. The sound scraped at Ruby's primal instincts, ramping up her fear.

"What about the howlers? They can't turn all the way, can they?"

"No, they can't. They didn't quite develop the way the king wanted. They're neither men nor wolf. But they may be useful soldiers if we can ever figure out how to control them."

They stood watching the beast in silence as it stalked around the cage. Ruby had run out of questions.

Normally, she would have been full of curiosity, but her mind was elsewhere. She could tell that the Huntsman was being indulgent with her because he wanted her to get used to being close to this monster.

She was going to have to fight one of these tonight.

And if she was really unlucky, she might even have to face a pack of them.

CHAPTER 16

$\mathcal{R}$uby sat in a wagon while the hunters drove deep into the woods. The path was rutted and rough, hardly a path at all. Few came through the woods, so it was a wonder that there was a wagon path to begin with.

Only those favored by the king were allowed to travel through the forest. There were old stories of kingdoms beyond the woods, but they were just children's tales told by grandmothers.

Ruby knew them all and tried to tell herself some of them to keep the panic at bay. There were stories of princes in lands of sunshine and happiness.

Stories of frogs and dwarves and happy endings. None of them helped her tonight. Instead, darker thoughts kept creeping in. Thoughts of poisoned apples, cursed spindles, and evil fairies.

And of course, stories of packs of wolfkin running through the villages under full moons, stealing children and dragging them into the woods.

The sky was darkening as night fell. It had still been light when they started. Ruby felt instantly disoriented as soon as she lost sight of the edge of the woods. Every tree looked alike in all directions.

The path was the only clue as to how to get back to the castle, but the ground was barely visible, and the path split countless times as they traveled. The Huntsman seemed sure of his way, though. He must have traveled through here many times to know the way in the fading light.

His men were less sure. They looked to the Huntsman at every juncture and waited until he pointed before turning in that direction. As they moved deeper and deeper into the forest, even the Huntsman's sense of direction must have been challenged, because he began to pause at every turn before deciding on a path.

Finally, they came to a place where the path simply disappeared into underbrush. Either they'd taken a wrong turn or they'd reached their destination.

Ruby could see that the men were wondering the same thing. But the Huntsman got off his horse with confidence, and that seemed to reassure everyone.

It was full night by then. The moonrise was barely beginning to lighten the sky. It would be a full moon tonight, and the Dark King would be holding his own nightmare hunt in this forest with other members of his court.

Ruby shivered at the thought. She didn't know which was worse—being run down like an animal by the king's noblemen or being bait for wild wolfkin.

The hunters moved gear and began setting up. They chopped branches and hid the wagons beneath them. Once every trace of man-made gear was hidden or carried, they found their positions. Many of them climbed trees along the path they'd just come from.

All of this was performed silently. They used the hand signals they'd practiced to communicate when they had to. But mostly, everyone knew their role and positions.

Ruby huddled in the center of the activity until it was her turn to act. She had only one role in this hunt.

She looked up at the hunters, trying to see where they'd gone. She'd seen them climb the trees and hide in bushes, but she couldn't make any of them out now.

They were there, though. All watching her. Ready to shoot at the first sign of attack.

It didn't quell her trembling or make her feel protected in the least. Their job was to catch the wolfkin, not to protect her from them. If she survived, it would be because of luck and her own fighting skill, not because the hunters were protecting her.

It was up to her to get out of the way of arrows and make sure she wasn't trapped in a net along with a wolfkin. She'd be as much in danger from the hunters as she was from the beasts.

She swallowed, but her throat was dry. She wished she could curl up in her cloak and disappear, but wishes wouldn't save her life tonight. So Ruby warmed her muscles by stretching and hopping. She couldn't risk having cold muscles when she could be fighting for her life at any moment.

Finally, it was time.

Out of the shadows, the trim shape of the Huntsman gave her the signal to move. Then he disappeared as if he was a shadow himself.

Ruby took a deep breath and picked up her basket. It was full of raw meat and fish, along with an open container of blood. Ruby was nothing but bait, so she supposed she was lucky that they didn't smear her with blood.

In the center of the basket was an extra knife. At least they'd armed her. Not that a few knives would do much against the power of a fiendish monster, but it was more than she'd had when she was captured in the woods during the Dark King's hunt.

She took another breath, trying to calm herself. She knew the men were waiting for her, but she dreaded starting this madness. What would they do if she simply refused to go anywhere?

An arrow shot from somewhere above and landed next to her. It stuck into the ground, angled toward the pathway, pointing to the direction she was supposed to go.

Ruby began walking slowly down the path.

CHAPTER 17

*T*yler watched as the girl walked down the path through the woods. She looked small and vulnerable, just as planned. Her fear was palpable and genuine.

That was an added bonus that always happened with the bait. The scent of fear would lure the wolfkin as much as the red cloak and blood.

If they were lucky, they'd capture a wolfkin tonight. If luck was truly with them, the wolfkin would eat the meat and fish in the girl's basket and then herd her to its den. They'd seen this behavior before, probably to eat the prey later or to feed its young.

In the past, Tyler and his hunters hadn't managed to track a wolfkin back to its den. The bait they'd used—a prisoner picked by the king himself—had died of his injuries before they reached the den. Rather than drag the body, the wolfkin had left the man and disappeared into the thicket.

In the end, the hunters had lost that wolfkin as well as the real prize. What they needed was someone strong and nimble enough to survive the initial attack. Someone who could stay alive until the wolfkin herded that person to its den.

Someone like this girl.

Everyone knew the stakes tonight. Tyler and his hunters had smeared dirt over themselves and did their best to stay upwind. Most of his men were stationed up in the trees, where the wolfkin were less likely to catch their scent.

Looking at the temptation that was this girl, Tyler was sure the beasts would be too distracted to notice his men. Live or die, she was going to be the best lure Tyler had ever used.

He wanted more than that, though. He wanted this one to survive. He had hopes of her being something more than just bait.

He found that he was breathing faster, and his hand was sweating from anticipation. Tyler frowned. After so many years of training, he was still nervous? How long had it been since he'd felt this way?

He wished he had Shadow with him. That dog had a way of calming him with his silly grin and mindless loyalty. Shadow had a simple kind of love and loyalty that Tyler had never found in a person. Even his father's love was complex and layered.

Tyler still remembered the time he'd tried to tell his father that he thought he might want to be a knight rather than a hunter. That was a cold month, when Tyler learned what it would be like to be without family.

Shadow wasn't here for the hunt yet. He had to stay with the other dogs back at the kennels. They were too noisy and aggressive to be part of a trap. Later, they'd be useful.

The dog handlers should be entering the forest about now with the dogs. Tyler looked forward to that stage of the game.

He took off his glove and wiped his hand dry on his pant

leg. He was confident that when the time came, his training would take over. It was the waiting that was hard.

Watching the girl walk alone in the woods stirred raw feelings in him that he didn't understand. Looking ever so vulnerable in her red cloak, she walked through Mathewson's area. Mathewson was the best of Tyler's men, and his men were the best there were, so the girl was as well protected as she could be.

She began humming.

The timid, trembling sound floated up to the branch where he perched. She was humming an old children's song —the one about going over the bridge and through the woods to Grandmother's house.

She was a young woman, but even when she fought for her life, she reminded him of a child sometimes. This was one of those times. He'd used how many baits now? Five? Six? This was the first one who'd hummed.

The sound was jerky and forced, not at all the cheerful song that little kids sang, but the heart of it was there. He hoped it kept up her courage.

A shadow shifted in the woods nearby. Was that the wind?

Twigs and dead leaves rustled to her right.

The girl stopped, spinning to look to her right.

Then she spun the other way, looking to her left.

She slowly turned, scanning the shadows and shifting branches around her.

Tyler strained his eyes and ears. His senses told him that it was just the wind and shifting moon shadows. But his hunter's instinct told him otherwise.

The wolfkin were here. Lurking in the shadows.

a rustling sound made the girl jerk back to the right. She backed up as something large came at her.

Tyler pulled his bow, ready to shoot as soon as he could see a target. But all he could see were shadows.

His muscles tensed at the sound of something large crashing through the underbrush.

A huge shape came barreling out of the shadows, making the girl yelp and jump out of the way.

It was a wagon.

It crashed into a tree and toppled onto its side with the wheels still spinning.

The wagon was one of Tyler's. The cage in the back was twisted and bent, as if the metal bars had been crushed beneath the weight of a boulder. But he would have heard it if there had been a smash big enough to bend metal.

A cold thought slithered through him. It hadn't been a boulder that had smashed and crushed the bars. It had been pure muscle—silent and full of fury as it twisted the metal.

Tyler didn't think a single wolfkin could do that, but all

the wolfkin he'd worked with at the castle were injured or damaged. He strained to see through the shadows.

The girl backed away from where the wagon had come from. She pulled the knife out of her basket, bloody and wet from being stored with the meat.

She was all eyes as she scanned the woods. Tyler could hear her breathing even from his perch high on his tree.

A scream shattered the night.

It came from one of the trees.

A vicious snarl joined the scream as the branches of a tree shivered and rocked.

Then a man fell out of his tree, flailing as he fell.

When he hit the ground, there was a thud as his bones broke. Moonlight shone on the hunter's lifeless face. It was Mathewson.

Tyler scanned Mathewson's tree, trying to see a target. He knew his men were doing the same.

All he saw were shadows of leaves shifting this way and that. All he heard was the sound of his own labored breathing in his ears.

Another scream.

It came from the underbrush. This time, it was more of a war cry than a surprised shock.

Tyler aimed his arrow at the mass of shadows where the sound came from.

One of his men leapt out of the shadows, desperately trying to escape. His face was covered in so much blood that Tyler couldn't tell who it was.

The injured man made it halfway out of the underbrush before his eyes went so wide that Tyler could see the whites in them.

Screaming and thrashing, the man was dragged back into the underbrush.

Tyler still couldn't see a target in the darkness, so he held his arrow. One of his men shot his, though.

The arrow disappeared into the darkness without a sound.

A moment later, the hunter who'd shot the arrow screamed. His branch rocked up and down, then shivered side to side.

Blood exploded out of the tree.

A severed leg dropped down.

It bounced and landed near the girl. She dropped her basket and hurriedly backed away from the leg, ending up by the broken wagon.

She held her knife before her like a talisman. The girl was the most optimistic soul Tyler had seen in a long time, if she thought she could fight off a full-blooded wolfkin with nothing but a knife.

Tyler fought the urge to slip down his tree and stand by her. It was a stupid urge, one that wouldn't help either of them. He could protect her far better from up here, which was why he'd stationed so many of his men in the trees.

His mind and instincts quarreled about whether to shoot. Anyone who shot an arrow would betray his position. He'd only have one shot before he had to move.

The woods were filling with snarls.

They'd attracted an entire pack of wolfkin.

CHAPTER 19

*R*uby held her knife before her as she scanned the area. The woods were full of screams and growls.

Her best chance at survival was to stay with the hunters. But the hunters were the ones screaming.

She couldn't see what was happening. The attacks were occurring all around her. She couldn't begin to guess how many wolfkin there were.

It sounded like they surrounded her. Enormous shadows leapt between the trees and disappeared in the underbrush.

Could she make it if she ran? Could she hide somewhere while the beasts were stalking the hunters?

She couldn't even finish the thought. Her instincts were too strong.

Ruby spun and ran.

She hadn't taken five steps before the air split with the sound of an enormous roar in front of her.

She spun and ran the other way.

This took her across the trail, where anyone and anything could clearly see her. But she had no choice. Ruby could almost feel the breath of the wolfkin behind her.

An arrow shot through the air, almost grazing her.

She didn't take the time to look back to see if it hit the target. She was almost to the other side of the wide trail.

Her path was blocked by a wagon flying through the air. It crashed into a tree and splintered.

Arrows flew everywhere now, but she couldn't stop running. Large, dark masses leapt along the edges of her sight.

Men screamed and beasts snarled. Warm blood splattered onto her face as she ran through the underbrush.

"Don't run!"

She thought she recognized the Huntsman's voice but couldn't be sure. It got drowned in the noise as she ran into the darkness of the woods.

Ruby ran as fast as she could. Jumping over logs and curving around trees. She was looking for a place to hide, but animals would be able to sniff her out if they were looking for her.

She needed to get far enough away that she could hide without being in the middle of a blood frenzy. But she couldn't run far. She knew better than to think she could outrun a wolfkin.

She found a shallow cave in a rock formation. The entrance was mostly covered by bushes. She wiggled her way in. It was more of a crevice than a cave—just barely big enough to hide her.

She curled into a ball, gripping her knife in front of her. The rock echoed her breathing around her. She tried to quiet it, but couldn't help the big, noisy gulps of air that her body refused to give up.

Her hands trembled as she waited. The sounds of men screaming their final cry of terror sounded far away, but she knew that the massacre was happening only a few steps away from her.

Ruby hadn't known that wolfkin could climb trees. It hadn't occurred to her that they could be smart enough to ambush the huntsmen. That was what it had been, hadn't it?

An ambush.

The wolfkin had understood that the hunters were setting a trap for them. Ruby should have been the easy kill, not the hunters.

When she closed her eyes, she saw that first wagon come tumbling down toward her. That had been a message. They understood what those wagons were used for—what the cages were used for.

They hadn't gone for the bait. They'd gone for the hunters.

All the stories she'd heard about the wolfkin being crazed animals were wrong. They might have been right about the domesticated ones that the Dark King owned. Any creature enslaved by the Dark King would probably be twisted and wrong.

But the wild ones, the natural wolfkin—they were like nothing she'd ever heard of before.

After a while, the screams subsided. The forest became quiet, with not a sound of rustling anywhere. No birds flew. No critters moved. It was as though the forest was holding its breath.

How long should she hide?

The immediate answer was to stay until daylight. But once the wolfkin were gone, the hunters—what was left of them—would come looking for her. She knew the hunting dogs were on their way. She'd heard the Huntsman talk about them. They would wait until the men had enough time to spring the trap, then the handlers would bring the dogs.

The original plan had been to hunt down any injured wolfkin, or perhaps to even try to find their den. The dogs would have been useful for that. But now, Ruby saw the hubris in that plan.

Dogs would find Ruby in no time. She wasn't that far from the hunters. If she wanted a shot at freedom, she needed to at least get out of the area. They might do a quick search for her, but she doubted they'd stay all night looking for her. They had their own injuries and the dead to tend to.

Her mind said to move farther away from the hunters, while her instincts told her to stay hidden. There were monsters out there. The hunters were nothing compared to the wolfkin.

She would stay hidden in this crevice.

As soon as she made up her mind, she began to feel better. Live or die, it was out of her hands now. There was a sort of comfort in knowing that there was nothing more for her to do.

She curled tighter and listened to her breathing, trying to quiet it.

Something rustled.

Ruby held her breath. Where had the sound come from?

Then she felt something cold slither along her leg.

In the dim light of the moon, she saw the arrow-shaped head of a snake slithering beside her.

Ruby clamped her mouth shut as she leapt out of the crevice in the rocks. She managed to swallow her scream, but couldn't keep herself from making a squealing, panicked sound as she crashed through the brush.

She frantically brushed her leg, making sure that the snake hadn't latched on. It hadn't, but her skin crawled as though it had.

Then she realized that she was standing out in the open. The moon shone down through the trees, beaming right at her.

Ruby felt, more than heard, the low growl that vibrated in her bones.

She was not alone.

When she looked up, she saw the wolfkin looking right at her.

CHAPTER 20

The girl was gone.

Tyler had watched her run. He'd even been foolish enough to yell down to her to not run, giving away his location to the monsters.

After that, he'd had to move out of his perch fast, before a wolfkin could find him. He stood on his branch, waiting a heartbeat or two to get his balance on the rocking branch.

One of the beasts was already snarling below him, leaping onto the lowest branch of Tyler's tree.

Tyler targeted a branch that looked large enough to hold him. It was farther away than he liked, but it wasn't an impossible distance.

One more heartbeat to steady his nerves, then he leapt from his branch.

He missed.

As he flew past his intended branch, he managed to grab another.

The branch jerked violently, threatening to snap under his weight. Hand over hand, he shimmied along the branch toward the trunk.

A wolfkin landed on his tree, shaking Tyler's world like a massive quake. Leaves rained on him, hiding the wolfkin as he leapt from branch to branch toward Tyler.

Tyler swung as hard as he could, getting momentum with his feet. He let go and flew toward the next tree.

He landed surprisingly well this time, grabbing a firm branch.

Luck was with him for the moment. Landing quietly made it harder for anything to track him. The forest was tight with trees growing so closely together that Tyler could jump to another tree.

He hadn't realized that wolfkin could climb.

There seemed to be a lot of things he didn't know about them, even after years of hunting them. But wolfkin were essentially canine. They might be supernatural and monstrous, but there was a limit. Trees were not their native territory.

The wolfkin that had been chasing him jumped down from his tree, looking for easier prey on the ground.

Three of Tyler's men lay on the ground, broken and bleeding. One was still alive and pleading for the gods to save him.

It was Smith. One of the youngest hunters. He was barely old enough to have hair on his chin, yet he had a wife and new baby waiting for him back home. He used to follow Tyler around the kennel when he was a child.

Two wolfkin pounced on Smith, snarling at each other. They tore him apart, each taking their half away to the underbrush.

Tyler closed his eyes, grudgingly allowing himself the luxury of not watching the torn body of his man be dragged away.

When it was over, all was quiet.

Tyler breathed silently, as he'd been trained to do his

whole life. But he couldn't calm the rage that roared through him.

There was no sign of the wolfkin.

He reminded himself that the surviving men relied on him to lead them with a clear head. They would wait for his cue before moving out of their hiding places.

After what seemed like a lifetime, Tyler finally climbed down from his tree. His muscles were stiff and bruised so he had to be extra careful not to fall. If the wolfkin were still around, there wouldn't be much he could do to save himself at this stage. A part of him wished for it, though. There was nothing he'd like better than to avenge his men.

Tyler stood in the clearing in the beams of moonlight for all to see. If the wolfkin were still here, they would attack him. And his men would know not to leave their hiding places.

Tyler looked around at the eerie forest. The crushed wagon lay on its side, splattered in gore. There wasn't much left of his fallen men. In addition to the three bodies he'd seen from above, he spotted the remains of another in the underbrush.

One by one, his men came down. That was the only way he could figure out who else had been killed. The remains were unidentifiable.

"We all knew the risks we were taking, lad." A large hand gripped Tyler's shoulder, adding some warmth to his cold body.

It should have been Mathewson who'd said that, but it was Clemens. He and Mathewson had been close. They were part of the old-timers who'd known Tyler as a boy. He wondered if Clemens realized yet that Mathewson was one of the fallen.

The rest of the men were silent. This wasn't the first time they'd lost good hunters, and it wouldn't be the last.

However, this was the first time they'd lost so many, and in such a horrific way.

It was as though the wolfkin had planned to ambush them. How could that be? No matter how clever the beasts were, they weren't human.

Tyler shook his head, bringing himself back to the task at hand. He and his men gathered the remaining wagons and loaded up the remains of the dead. It was such a disturbing job that he wondered if it would be better just to leave the fallen where they were.

But of course, that would be abandoning his hunters to the night creatures of the forest. There were rituals that needed to be performed for both the dead and the living. As hard as this was for him and his men, it would be far harder for the families.

So they gathered the remains with as much respect as they could. The horses were either gone or killed, so they had to wait until the dog handlers arrived.

When they did, they hitched the horses to the remaining cage wagon and drove it back to the castle with the men. There wasn't enough room to take all the men, so half of them had to wait until the first group brought back the wagon. Nobody wanted to be left here in the woods.

Nobody except Tyler.

"Come here, boy." Tyler put his hand out to Shadow, who trotted over to him.

The dog licked Tyler's face, comforting him in a way that nothing else could. Shadow wasn't one of the working dogs, but as Tyler's personal pet, he often came on the hunts. Tonight, Tyler had made sure that Shadow would come. He knew the girl's scent better than any of the other dogs.

"Find the girl," Tyler told Shadow.

Shadow whined and sat.

"What's the girl's name?" asked Tyler.

"Ruby," said Clemens.

A jewel of a name for a jewel of a girl. He should have known. She would probably have been treasured, if life had been different for her.

"Ruby," said Tyler. "Shadow, find Ruby."

Shadow—being the brave, loyal, amazing and stupid dog that he was—ran without hesitation into the dark forest.

Tyler replenished his arrows, then followed his dog into the woods.

CHAPTER 21

*R*uby ran for her life.

Through the streams, over the fallen logs, and around gullies. She fell and slid along dead leaves and dirt all the way down a ravine. That hurt all over, but she lost the wolfkin for the moment.

Up until now, they'd chased her, one on either side of her as she ran. They were powerful creatures and could have caught her whenever they wished. But they didn't.

Instead, they ran with her. Were they toying with her? Were they training one of their young?

She trudged up a stream, trying to clear her scent trail. After a while, a tiny, fragile flame of hope began to glow inside her. Maybe she'd lost them.

Ruby veered off from the stream and walked away from the water. She was completely lost and had nothing to lead her. She could see the moon, but it rose and set at different places during different times of the year, and she'd never paid attention to those patterns. Gran had always said it was important to pay attention to everything, but there was so much, and even Gran had let the moon lessons slide for another time.

Gran would know what to do and which direction to go. Ruby sighed. She'd have to pick a path and hope for the best.

She walked for a while, trying not to notice that all the trees looked alike. She tried even harder not to wonder if she was walking in a giant circle.

A low growl came from her left.

Ruby froze, trying to be silent.

The growl became louder and came toward her.

She turned and ran.

Over and over, Ruby slowed down, thinking that she'd lost the beasts. She would walk for a while longer, then she'd hear the growl again. Sometimes, the sound would come from her left, sometimes from her right.

Each time, Ruby ran as fast and far away as she could. She couldn't keep it up forever, though. At some point, she'd have to hide or stand her ground and fight.

Her experience with the snake made her reluctant to find another hiding spot. But fighting a wolfkin wasn't a good option either, especially since she was exhausted. Ruby walked when she could and ran when she had to, and eventually had no choice but to look for a decent hiding spot.

She found that there was no place to hide in this part of the forest—no rock formations, no big bushes. There was hardly any underbrush here. It was just big trees everywhere she looked.

The moon was on the other side of the sky by the time Ruby could no longer run. She trudged through the woods, knowing that if a beast came at her now, she would have no choice but to stand there like a frightened rabbit. She was wondering whether she could climb a tree to rest when she saw the most miraculous thing.

A flickering light.

Ruby blinked rapidly, trying to reassure herself that she was really seeing it. It looked like the light of a lantern.

A surge of energy rose in her and she stumbled toward the light.

The woods thinned as she ran. The ground became more packed. And the single lantern light became a window of a cottage.

Ruby stepped out of the forest and into a field. From here, she could see small cottages dotting the outskirts of the village.

She shook with tears that crushed her chest and weakened her knees. The relief was such a strong wave that it almost hurt.

She stumbled toward the cottages with her breath catching. There was nothing to stop a wolfkin from leaping out of the forest and snatching her in the field, so she moved as fast as her exhausted legs would carry her.

When she reached the first cottage, she recognized it. She was not far from her grandmother's house. She had to pause in wonder at her luck.

Gran had always said for her to trust her instincts. Yet Ruby knew that her instincts in the forest were terrible. She had no idea where she was going. She was too panicked to even pay attention to her direction when the wolfkin were nearby.

Yet here she was. Exactly where she'd longed to be.

She was both crying and laughing as she walked to her grandmother's house.

CHAPTER 22

*T*yler searched the crevice in the rocks for any sign that Shadow might truly have Ruby's scent. The dog dug into the crevice, excited about something. He backed out of the narrow cave with a snake in his jaws.

Shadow shook it, practically tearing it to pieces. Then he dropped the dead snake at Tyler's feet.

Tyler looked at his grinning dog. Shadow looked proud of himself with his tongue lolling out of the side of his mouth.

"We've lost enough hunters tonight," said Clemens. His voice was emotionless. He must have realized by now that Mathewson was one of the missing. "Let's go. The wagon is probably back by now."

Clemens and a couple of other men had followed Tyler into the woods. They must have been terrified and rattled by the night's events. Yet they still followed him deeper into hell.

His men were as loyal and foolishly courageous as Shadow. Tyler couldn't risk them any more than he already had.

They all knew that tonight, they were the ones being

hunted. Traumatized and exhausted, the last thing they needed was to stumble into the wolfkin den.

Tyler didn't even know why he was so set on getting this girl—Ruby—back. It couldn't be concern for her. She'd been meant from the start to be offered up as bait.

There was no chance of Ruby surviving, no matter how good of a fighter she was. The slaughter tonight had been too vicious, too organized for there to be much hope of the beasts carrying her off to their lair. The attack hadn't been about food—it had been an all-out war.

Even if everything had gone according to plan, it would have been ridiculous to expect...what? That she'd join them as a hunter? That she'd help Tyler capture enough wolfkin to give the Dark King what he wanted?

"Come, Shadow."

It was time to give up on this foolishness. Shadow didn't have Ruby's scent anyway.

Tyler turned and walked back toward the clearing where his men had been massacred. Strangely, giving up on finding Ruby felt like he was losing another one of his hunters.

CHAPTER 23

The king rarely slept. Through the long night, his nobles and servants were expected to be available for business and entertainment whenever the king wished. That also meant that, no matter how late the hour, Tyler had to give his report on his so-called hunt as soon as he arrived back at the castle.

He did not bother to bathe or change into clean clothes. Any delay would annoy the king for he was always eager to hear details of Tyler's hunts. The last thing he wanted was to give the king any further reason to be annoyed.

So Tyler walked into the king's personal chambers with dried blood still splattered on his face. The Dark King smiled when he saw it.

"You've come fresh from your hunt, I see." The king took off his gloves, which were as bloody as Tyler's.

"Yes, Your Majesty."

The king sat on a chair, letting his valets take his muddy boots off. "I'm in a good mood, Tyler. The Midnight Hunt tonight was invigorating." The king thumped his fist against his chest. "Everyone needs to be in touch with his savage self, don't you think?"

"Yes, Your Majesty."

"So, did you catch me a wolfkin tonight?"

"I'm afraid not, Your Majesty." Tyler braced for the king's reaction.

The king's good mood vanished as he threw his gloves down on the rug. His valets cringed a little, looking like they wanted to disappear.

"It's been months since you caught me a wild wolfkin, and the one you did catch still isn't trained. How am I to…" The king looked down at his valets. "You two, get out."

The valets hopped up and scurried out of the king's chambers as quickly as they could.

"Damn spies," said the king. "I'd have them all executed if I didn't know that she'd just replace them with worse. At least these spies are stupid and afraid of me."

Tyler didn't want to know who the king thought would be spying on him. The king had executed his last queen years ago and hadn't remarried.

"Those valets have been your loyal servants for years, Your Majesty."

"And yet she still managed to turn them against me. She's hardly pretending anymore." Spittle sprayed from the king's mouth as he paced near his bed.

Tyler did not want to ask who "she" was. If the king wanted him to know, he'd tell him. Tyler had learned at an early age that it was better to stay out of court politics if at all possible. Sometimes, even knowing the name of a royal enemy could be fatal, especially if they became allies again.

There were rumors, though, that the king hated the prince's wife. But if that had been true, the king would simply have executed her, so it was difficult to entirely believe. Still, the Dark King's court had layers upon layers of intrigue, and even the king sometimes couldn't do what he wanted. Anything was possible.

"She has everyone in this castle fooled," said the king. "But not me. She's trying to usurp my power, but I won't let her." The king thumped his chest with a large fist. "I'll stuff her right back into a wraith horse where she belongs. I'll cut out a patch of her skin and wear it on my cloak."

The king stepped close to Tyler and lowered his voice. "I need that army. Not next year, not in six months. *Now*."

"Yes, Your Majesty."

The king had never told Tyler why he needed the army of wolfkin. Tyler used to assume that the king wanted it simply as a show of power, but lately, there had been an urgency about his demands that suggested otherwise.

Before the prince got married, the king seemed to want nothing more than his usual dark entertainment and to find a bride for his heir. But ever since the prince's wedding, all he ever talked about was getting an army of wolfkin to protect his kingdom. There were many who'd begun to whisper of him as the Mad King rather than the Dark King.

"Tell me how it went, Huntsman. It must have gone bad— otherwise, you would have announced your victory already."

Tyler gathered his thoughts. If his report came out wrong, it could be the last words he ever uttered.

"We were ambushed. We lost four good hunters."

"Ambushed by who?"

"The wolfkin, Your Majesty."

The king sat back and looked out the window at the moon. It looked like the old soldier in him was calculating something.

"They understood what the cage wagons were used for. They pinpointed our men as soon as we shot arrows, and they climbed trees to get at us."

"You mean to tell me they can think? Coordinate like hunters and execute an attack?"

"It would seem so, Your Majesty."

"They can climb trees? Could they scale a castle wall, do you think?"

"Possibly."

The king barked a laugh. He got up and walked over to the window in his bare feet. The moonlight bathed him, highlighting the different colored patches of his robe.

People said his robe was made of the various skins of his fallen enemies. The rumors were that they were wild fairy skin from the Wild Wars that made him king. It was true that some of those patches were blue, orange, and mottled purple, but most of it had the varying colors of human flesh.

"Bring me more wolfkin, Huntsman. I want at least three wild ones to begin with. And this time, don't fail me."

"Yes, Your Majesty." Tyler bowed, bracing for the threat that he knew would come.

"How is your father, Tyler?"

And there it was.

"He is…still alive. Thank you for asking, Your Majesty."

"I do like to keep an eye on my subjects. Your father is especially interesting to me. I should hate to see the poor man struggle more than he already has."

Tyler bowed, as was expected. He couldn't utter another "Your Majesty," not while being threatened.

"It's a shame, isn't it? Of all the people that such misfortune could strike, it had to be your father. You know, he used to be my best hunter. I'm glad he had a healthy, *normal* son like you to take his place when he failed me one too many times. Do you have any children, Huntsman?"

"No, Your Majesty."

"Shame. I suppose you were too young for that when you inherited your father's job. You won't have time to have one now until you get me what I want. Go. And don't come back until you can show me the wolfkin that you've caught for me."

Tyler bowed again as he left, trying not to show the rage that bubbled in him.

CHAPTER 24

A warm glow spilled out from the windows of Ruby's grandmother's house. The colorful flowers that grew all over the yard was lit by its warmth.

Gran was the only one in the village who could grow flowers. For everyone else, they wilted and came out colorless, listless. But for Gran, the flowers burst with color all year long.

The garden looked wild and weedy, which was unusual. The flowers were there, but many of them were closed now. Even Silver the Flower Peddler couldn't keep the flowers open during the long nights, no matter how much her wealthy customers complained.

Flowers were a luxury that only the wealthy could afford. So it was easy to spot Gran's house, since the yard was full of flowers that even the wealthiest merchant would have trouble affording.

Ruby ran to the door of the small cottage and knocked on the door.

"Gran, it's me, Ruby."

All she could hear were the sounds of crickets and frogs.

"Gran, it's me. Let me in."

Ruby had expected her grandmother to come rushing to the door with tears in her eyes. She had no idea how long it had been since she'd been dragged out of her father's house for the Dark King's hunt. It felt like a lifetime ago.

If Ruby had gone to her father first, he wouldn't have known what to do with her. He had been too afraid to even fight the soldiers when they took Ruby from him. She was afraid he'd die of fright if he saw her now.

Maybe her grandmother was out? It was in the middle of the night, so Ruby couldn't imagine where Gran might be. She wasn't too worried, though, because she could see the fire in the fireplace. Gran sometimes went off on mysterious errands, often coming back with cuts and bruises. Wherever Gran was, she would be back.

Ruby tried the door. It opened. Everyone in Midnight locked their doors, but Gran had a reputation and usually didn't need to worry about that sort of thing.

Ruby walked into her grandmother's cottage like a sleep-walker. She couldn't believe she was here. She began to tremble all over and nearly collapsed onto Gran's rocking chair in front of the fireplace.

There was a pot of soup simmering over the fire. The scent of the meat and garden vegetables filled her nose. Only Gran's soup could get her to drag herself out of the rocking chair, but the scent was irresistible.

Ruby ladled soup into a bowl and marveled at the warm flavor of a slow-cooked meal. The warm broth was like magic flowing through her body—relaxing every part of her, including her stomach, which had been tense and churning for far too long.

When she was done, Gran still hadn't come home. Ruby sat in the rocking chair by the fire. She couldn't remember the last time she felt this relaxed.

Listening to the fire crackling and the crickets chirping, she dozed off in the rocking chair.

The sound of the door opening brought Ruby out of a deep sleep. Tears welled in Ruby's eyes as she saw her grandmother's familiar shape filling the doorway.

Gran's silver hair was pulled back in the same bun she always had it in. Her shiny eyes looked at her with warmth and love. Her arms opened to welcome Ruby.

Ruby rushed into her grandmother's arms and began sobbing. Gran held her and rocked her gently the way she used to when Ruby was little. She quietly closed the door and walked Ruby to her chair in front of the fireplace.

Ruby shook all over as she sat in front of the warm fire.

Gran made tea and handed it to Ruby. The warmth felt so good in Ruby's hands and throat as she drank it.

Gran didn't press for details. She just quietly moved about the dim kitchen, tidying the table.

"Where were you?" asked Ruby.

"I was looking for you."

"Me? It's the middle of the night. And I've been gone for a long time."

"I was worried sick about you all that time, you know. I would have done anything to get you out of that horrible castle." Gran folded a cloth and began wiping the table.

"You knew I was in the castle?"

Gran paused in her wiping. There was a moment that piqued Ruby's interest. What was her grandmother thinking about? Whatever it was, she didn't want Ruby to know.

"I didn't know where you were at first, of course," said Gran. "I searched in the forest every day, calling for you until my voice became hoarse."

Ruby took in a sharp breath. "In the forest? You shouldn't have done that, Gran. Who knows what kind of monsters might have caught you? The wild fairies—"

"You don't need to remind me of the wild fairies, child. I'm the one who told you about them before you could even walk."

"I'm glad you're all right," said Ruby.

"I'm glad you're safe too." Gran walked around the table and hugged Ruby again.

Ruby had been so steeped in her own situation that it hadn't occurred to her that any of her family could have been in danger while she was away. She couldn't imagine the world without her grandmother.

"Gran, your training saved my life."

"That was the whole point, little one. Although I had hoped that you'd never need to use it."

"I used it all the time. It kept me alive." Ruby didn't say that it kept her safe. That was a word that she could never use when she talked about her time in the castle.

There had been cruel guards there, as well as other men who thought they could do whatever they wanted with people who were weaker than them. They all learned to stay away from Ruby.

The guards were bigger and better fed, but they were nowhere near as well trained as Ruby. Most of them had almost no training at all. They relied on their numbers and the fear of the king's authority.

If they'd ganged up on her, they would have beaten her. Ruby was keenly aware that it was just a matter of time before they decided to do that. But in the meantime, she did her best to entertain the other guards with a good fight.

Over time, Ruby ended up having better training than even what her grandmother could have given her. There was nothing better than a real fight with her life at stake to sharpen her skills. She earned a reputation as the skinny girl who could beat a guard twice her size. Sometimes two. That reputation had been both good and bad.

When a new guard or a new bully came into the laborer's pool, the other guards and bullies would needle them into attacking Ruby. Then the bets on how long the fight would last would begin. So long as Ruby could entertain the group, she could keep that delicate balance of staying alive.

It was just a matter of time before one of her beaten opponents had enough pull to get her picked to be thrown into the dungeons. No one ever came back from the dungeons.

"I know we have a lot to talk about," said Gran. Her keen eyes told Ruby that she understood at least some of Ruby's thoughts. "But you need your rest. We'll talk in the morning, shall we?"

Ruby nodded. She was so exhausted and relieved that she couldn't imagine getting up out of this warm chair. She just let her grandmother take care of her the way she used to when she was little. Gran had always been mother and father, trainer and teacher. Even though Ruby lived with her father, he had always been a minor figure in her life compared to Gran.

Ruby was almost asleep by the time Gran wrapped a blanket around her. Being in her grandmother's home was nothing but pure joy.

Ruby barely had that thought before her eyelids slid down and she fell asleep in her chair.

CHAPTER 25

*R*uby woke up with sunlight in her eyes. The sun set early these days, but it never seemed to rise any later—or at least it never felt like it. For once, though, the day was bright, and the dried flowers around the cottage were colored so intensely that they almost didn't look real.

She looked around groggily, her memories mixed for a moment.

Then she remembered that she was in her grandmother's house.

Her back was stiff and so was her neck. She'd fallen asleep in the chair by the fire, and Gran hadn't woken her up to put her to bed.

Gran's cottage looked the same as it always had. There were dried flowers everywhere, adding color to the place in a way that was unheard of in a villager's home.

The long nights threatened the flower business, but that seemed to only have made the smaller crop of flowers even more valuable. The last time Ruby had helped Gran with her flower stand, there had been nobles willing to spend almost any amount to show their status by buying something as frivolous and expensive as flowers.

Gran's cottage was rich with glorious color. Even though flowers were precious, no one dared to steal any of her flowers out of her yard. It would be obvious that, unless you were a noble, anyone who had flowers in their home must have stolen them.

People might have stolen flowers anyway, but Silver the Flower Peddler had a bit of a reputation. None of the villagers wanted to cross her, not even the would-be flower pirates who might have undersold Gran.

Normally, Gran kept a tidy house to display the precious flowers. But not today.

Today, there was dirt and dried mud all over the floor. It was very unlike Gran to allow anyone to track mud into her cottage.

Ruby stretched and yawned, loving the sensation of being home. She had practically grown up here.

Thoughts of the forest and her life as a captive tried to take over, but Ruby would have none of it. At least for now, she was determined to enjoy being safe.

She was alive. Ruby shook her head at the wonder of that.

She walked over to the corner where the broom leaned and began to sweep, careful not to make noise. Gran must be still asleep in the other room.

Sweeping was one of the many ways Ruby wanted to thank Gran. Her grandmother would know what to do and how to hide Ruby. Gran had more experiences than Ruby could imagine. She always seemed to know what to do, even in the direst situations.

As she swept, Ruby noticed some unusual marks on the floor. There were large tracks in the dried mud.

Lines that looked like claw marks.

They weren't long, but they were all over the floor, as though a large animal had walked through.

Ruby's skin prickled along her arms. She bent down to look closely at the markings.

The tracks led from the back door and were all over the cottage.

Ruby stood up slowly, trying to fathom what it could mean. Had there been a dog in here?

If so, it had been one enormous dog. Besides, Gran didn't like animals in her house. Ruby was about to begin sweeping again when she saw the paw print.

That was no dog. Ruby could step into the print with both her feet and still see the outline of it. Her heart thudded loudly in her chest.

She glanced over at the closed door to the other room. People assumed it was the bedroom, and they were half right. Gran did often sleep there. But Ruby had never thought of it as a bedroom, particularly since Gran slept on the floor in a bedroll as though she was still a soldier, out sleeping by the open fire.

Ruby had grown up thinking of that room as the armory. When she was little, she'd thought that all grandmothers had an armory in their homes. It wasn't until she was older when she realized that Gran wasn't like the other grandmothers.

Ruby would have heard something if there had been an attack here. She had been exhausted, but she hadn't been dead to the world. She was tempted to wake her grandmother and ask her if she was all right.

She resisted the urge. Her life in the barn had been a violent one, and she'd lived with fear far too long. Gran used to tell Ruby stories of soldiers coming back from the battles during the Wild Wars. Many of them came back traumatized and couldn't adapt back to normal village life.

Ruby looked at her hand. It had a slight tremor. She fisted it to stop the shaking.

That must be it. Ruby was going through what soldiers went through after a battle. She'd be all right. Not everything was a life-threatening situation.

She took another look at the paw print. It certainly looked like a print, but Gran sometimes got requests for flower arrangements in fanciful pottery. There was no telling what a noblewoman might want for a theme party. Besides, if a wolfkin ever came in here, the place would look like a hurricane went through it.

There was no place safer than her grandmother's house.

Ruby took a deep breath and let it out slowly, counting flowers as she exhaled. By the time she took the next breath, she felt calmer. No one was attacking her at this moment, and that was what mattered.

Whatever had happened here was done. The mud was dried and there were no bloodstains on the floor. Gran had seemed tired but fine last night. Of course, Ruby had been in no condition to notice details.

She'd have plenty of time to ask Gran what happened to cause all this mess later. She didn't need to wake her over this.

Ruby continued to sweep the floor. She realized after a while that some part of her had been looking for Gran's footsteps in the dried mud.

She swept the whole house, but never found them.

CHAPTER 26

*B*y the time Gran finally came into the room, the sun had been up for hours. Ruby had been on the verge of going into the armory to wake her up. But when Gran finally showed up, it wasn't from the armory. It was through the back door.

"How long have you been up?" asked Ruby.

Gran had grass in her hair and stains on her dress. That wasn't so unusual. She always worked outside in the dirt and flowers. What was unusual was that her hair was down. Her silver locks were tangled and cascading over her shoulders.

And she was barefoot. There was dirt and bits of dried mud on her feet.

"What happened to your shoes?"

Gran looked down at her feet. "Oh, I must have lost them somewhere."

Ruby frowned. "Are you all right?" She steered her grandmother to sit on a bench.

"I'm fine, child. You don't have to treat me like an old woman."

"Then don't act like one. Where were you?"

"I was training."

"Barefoot?"

"Sometimes, one must train barefoot. You should try it."

Ruby sat on the bench beside Gran. "Why was the floor so muddy?"

Gran glanced at Ruby. That look told her that the old soldier was still in her grandmother. It was cold and calculating, and it made Ruby want to sit a little farther away from her.

"You noticed. I taught you well."

"Yes, you did. And it kept me alive. Thank you. Now, please tell me what is happening."

Her grandmother looked her right in the eyes and said, "A neighbor's dog. I was just too tired to clean it up. I see you did a nice job of sweeping. How about breakfast?"

Gran got up and started to rummage around in the kitchen.

"Aren't you going to ask me where I was and what happened?" asked Ruby.

"Certainly. You can tell me as I cook."

But Ruby could tell that she already knew at least some of it. That didn't shock Ruby. Gran knew a lot of things that most people would never know. Something was not right, though, and Ruby needed some time to think about it.

"Let's talk while we eat," said Ruby. "I'm tired and need a little sunshine."

Ruby went out the front door and sat on the stairs. She left the door open so that she could hear Gran clanging about in the kitchen.

Ruby sat in the sun, soaking up the warmth, while she watched her grandmother through the open door. The iron pots and pans were heavy, but Gran seemed to have no trouble working with them. In fact, she lifted them up as though they were as light as a breeze.

Gran didn't bother to clean her dirty feet or put shoes on. She left dirt sprinkled all over her floor as she moved about.

Something was going on. Whatever it was, Ruby found a strange comfort in knowing that Gran wasn't trying very hard to hide things from her.

The woman was an expert in intrigue in every sense of the word. She'd never outright said it, but Ruby suspected that Gran had been a spy for at least some of her missions during the Wild Wars.

If she really wanted to hide something from Ruby, she wouldn't go about it like this. So what did that mean? Why would Gran hide something but not hide it at the same time? Was she trying to tell Ruby something? Something that she worried might be too much of a shock?

"Gran, you didn't seem that surprised to see me last night."

"That's because I have big ears to hear you with, my dear. I could hear you rustling about inside the cottage."

Ruby frowned. "Were you expecting me? How did you know it was me?"

"Who else would walk into my cottage in the middle of the night? Besides, I also have big eyes to see you with and a window to peer through."

Gran was talking strangely. It didn't sound like her.

"Your ears and eyes must be pretty great to know that it was me. You haven't seen me in ages."

"Truth be told, I haven't slept well since they took you. I spent every night hoping you'd show up at my door. I never stopped looking for you, you know. I even went deep into the forest to places I'd never gone before."

"You shouldn't do that, Gran. It's too dangerous."

Gran didn't reply to that. She was the one who'd taught Ruby about the dangers of the dark forest. If the wild fairies didn't get you, the wolfkin surely would.

"Did you see any of the wild fairies or wolfkin?" asked Ruby.

"I did my best not to stray too far during the full moons."

That didn't answer the question.

"How do you survive spending so much time in the woods, Gran?"

"The way I did during the Wild Wars." She sounded sad. "I let go a piece of my humanity. That always seems to be the price for survival."

Wind blew from the forest, brushing its cold fingers along the back of Ruby's neck.

CHAPTER 27

*T*yler had to be the one to tell his hunters' families that the man they loved was not ever coming home.

He could have written a letter and had someone read it to them. Or sent a royal messenger to deliver the news on behalf of the king. Or spent the day going for a walk with Shadow to gather his thoughts and plan out his next move.

But he felt that telling the families himself was necessary to show respect and tribute to the good men who had died. He stood like a rock and let the wives pound on his chest and slap him. He watched one father crumple to the ground when he heard that his only child had been killed.

Tyler patiently answered questions about how they died and what went wrong. He generalized as best he could, trying to spare the families the gruesome details. When they pressed him for specifics, he lied when he had to—telling them that their loved one died painlessly and that their death allowed the rest of the group to accomplish their mission.

He knew from too much experience that the families needed to hear that the death of their loved one wasn't meaningless, even though it always was. He always made sure they knew that their father, husband, or son died bravely and with honor.

He also made sure that the families continued to get the wages that the dead man used to bring into the family. It was the least he could do.

Soon, Tyler would have a full roster of ghost hunters who drew wages. At some point, the king's coin counters would notice and demand that he stop this practice. Until then, Tyler would keep it up. It helped that the king had commanded that the Huntsman get whatever he needed to catch the wolfkin. So few bothered to look closely at his spending.

When he was done with telling the families the horrible news, he stood out in the sun. The warmth felt good on his skin. Little by little, his muscles began to relax.

This was not the first time he'd had to deliver terrible news, but this was the first time he'd had to visit so many families in one day. When he closed his eyes, he saw tears streaking down the crumpled faces of broken families. Many of them were from children who would never see their fathers again.

Tyler sighed. It was time to go see his own father.

He walked over to the kennels first. He often left Shadow there instead of leaving him in his personal chambers. Shadow had company in the kennels, which was much better than him moping about alone indoors.

Tyler's dog was not the best company when visiting grieving families. He tried to protect Tyler from the slaps and yelling, and that only added to the drama. Tyler deserved everything he got. These people had entrusted their men to Tyler's care and leadership. And he had failed them.

Shadow was no good for visits to his father, either, but he was good company on the way there and back.

As usual, his dog was overjoyed to see him. That silly pup was the only creature in the world who was happy to see Tyler. It always amazed him how consistent Shadow's welcome was. His love was unconditional and simple in a way that no human relationship ever was.

Tyler was in no mood for adoration, though. But he kneeled and rubbed Shadow's coat because it made the dog so happy. Shadow rolled onto his back and Tyler rubbed his belly.

His dog squirmed happily. After a few moments, Tyler reluctantly relaxed. It was hard to be tense around so much simple joy.

As the king's huntsman, Tyler was in charge of many animals, including dogs. They all had their roles in the big menagerie that the king kept.

Shadow, as capable as he could be, simply didn't have the killer discipline of Tyler's hunting dogs. But he brightened Tyler's day, and that was worth more than gold in the Kingdom of Midnight.

"If I was king, you'd be my jester." Tyler stood up, brushing his hands on his trousers. "Come on, Shadow. Let's go see our sire."

They walked through the kennels and into the castle kitchen. Tyler collected a platter with his father's lunch and managed to get a bone for Shadow too. He didn't give the bone to Shadow right away, much to the dog's distress.

Tyler didn't feel so bad about that, though, as Shadow should know the routine by now. He was just acting like a puppy.

That was Tyler's fault. He was far too indulgent with Shadow. But it gave him the chance to sometimes spoil his dog in a way that he couldn't with his work animals.

The gloom that usually settled on him as he neared his father was particularly heavy today. Perhaps he should have let someone else handle his father's lunch. It had been a hard day, and he didn't have a lot left to deal with his father.

But Tyler was determined to keep a connection with his father alive—no matter how thin it was. So he walked to the tall fence of his father's yard and dropped the bone for Shadow. His dog happily lay down and began gnawing on it. It was a large bone with some bits of meat and gristle still attached, which would occupy him for some time.

Shadow got agitated around Tyler's father, which in turn agitated his father. Tyler had learned quickly to keep those two apart.

He walked past the fence and into the open yard where his father sat. The fence served no purpose other than to keep the workers from gawking at his father. Tyler knew there was nothing he could do to keep the rumors down, but at least his hunters had enough respect not to gossip.

His father leapt up as soon as Tyler walked into his yard and watched him approach.

"Hello, Father." Tyler kept his voice gentle and cautious, just as he had with the dead men's families. "I brought you lunch."

His father made a low noise that was almost animal. It cut Tyler's heart to hear it. Would it ever get easier?

Tyler uncovered the platter to show his father the pile of meat.

His father gripped the metal bars of his cage, salivating at the plate.

Tyler always hated this next part. He grabbed the stick lying on the ground beside the cage and poked it into his father's belly, gently pushing him back.

"You know the drill, Father. You'll get your lunch when you back away enough to let me put it in your cell."

This was the time when Tyler always held his breath in

hope, in anticipation. After all this time, he still felt himself holding his breath.

But Father did not back away. He pressed himself into the stick, rattling his cage and making inhuman sounds until Tyler was forced to smack him enough to back away.

His father always had been the most stubborn man he'd ever met. When Father finally backed away, Tyler smacked the platter against the bars, dumping his father's lunch onto the floor of the cage.

Father jumped on the food as soon as the raw meat hit the ground.

Tyler watched his father grab the meat with his teeth as he leaned over on all fours.

His body was hairy, but not so hairy as an animal's. His fingers were stunted, but still identifiable as fingers. It was the face that bothered Tyler the most. The jaws were elongated like a snout, but the eyes were still that of his father's.

It would be easier if Tyler couldn't recognize his father anymore. Then he wouldn't be reminded of the times when he used to ride his father's shoulders as a child, or hear his voice as he taught young Tyler the thousands of things that a Huntsman must know.

Tyler sat on the bench nearby and began to tell his father about his day.

CHAPTER 28

"The war is heating up," said Gran in a low voice. "Your time of childhood will soon be over."

Ruby paused her forkful of eggs on its way to her mouth. She was tempted to put it down, to start the old argument again, but what was the point?

"I'm not a child anymore."

"Every child thinks that. The way to tell if your childhood is over is if you start to miss it instead of being smug about having outgrown it. When that happens, then you'll know it's over."

Ruby continued to eat, chewing thoughtfully on her eggs. "How are the flowers doing?"

"They're struggling with these long nights, but you don't care a fig about my flowers. I'm sorry to say that you'll have to hear me talk about the war, whether you like it or not."

Her grandmother was the most amazing person Ruby had ever met. But Gran and her old cronies lived in a fantasy world of intrigue and war that had been over since before Ruby had been born. Only the old-timers ever talked about the Wild Wars anymore.

"You don't want to hear my report of what happened to me while I was gone?" Ruby was a tiny bit hurt that Gran was more interested in ancient history than what Ruby had been through.

They'd always made a game of Ruby reporting as many details as she could to Gran. It had been one of the ways they had bonded. That and the fight training.

Ruby had been content to let her grandmother train her as a spy and soldier. It was a way of connecting with her and even acknowledging Gran's beliefs about the supposedly ongoing war, without ever agreeing with or contradicting her about it.

Ruby's favorite game as a child had been to pretend that she was on a mission. Gran would give her one, and Ruby would run off to accomplish it.

It used to be fun. Until Ruby became old enough to understand that to Gran, it was more than just a game.

"Of course I'm interested in your report," said Gran. "I'm more interested than you can imagine. But it's time for you to understand why."

Ruby kept chewing mechanically. She concentrated on spearing a piece of tomato.

"I can see you have no interest in what I have to say," said Gran.

"When are you going to move on, Gran? Fairies are noblemen's slaves now, not our enemies. The war is over. It has been my whole life. If you keep talking like this, Father will end up putting you away and taking over your flower business."

Gran snorted. "That pasty boy couldn't nurture a weed, much less flowers that nobles would want gracing their ballrooms."

"That's not the point. The point is that if you behave oddly enough and talk too much nonsense, they'll—"

"Were the trainers impressed with your fighting skills?"

Ruby put down her fork. "How did you know—"

"Will they be brave enough to go back into the forest, do you think?"

Ruby stared at her grandmother. Hadn't the Huntsman told her that his hunt was a secret?

"How do you feel about going back to Midnight Castle?"

That jarred Ruby out of her stupor. "*What?*"

"Not as a prisoner this time."

"I don't want to ever go back to that horrible place."

"Even if you were to go there on a mission?"

Ruby rubbed her face, trying to gather her thoughts. Gran looked the way she always had—strong, capable, beautiful with her silver hair and graceful body. She'd always been sensible, the emotional pillar of strength that Ruby had relied on her entire life.

Now, Ruby wasn't so sure. She took Gran's hand in hers.

"No matter what you think, I'm not a child anymore. Your training saved my life, but we're not spies in a war, Gran. The evil in this kingdom is caused by our own king, not by wild fairies."

"Open your eyes. The king does not have the power to chase away the sun early each day. The signs are here— daylight getting shorter every day, the two extra moons that appeared just before they dragged you away, the strange stories coming from the Dark Castle since the prince's royal wedding. Why do you think the king is so desperate to capture wolfkin?"

Ruby could only stare at her. She hadn't told Gran about the wolfkin.

"Have you known all this time where I was and what was happening at the Dark Castle?"

Gran sighed and nodded.

Ruby couldn't help the hurt and accusation in her eyes.

"I couldn't get you out. You know that. No one can just walk into the Dark Castle and walk out with one of the king's prisoners."

"Then how did you know what was happening to me?"

"I have friends, who have friends. We talk."

Ruby lowered her voice. "You have people in the castle?"

"You make it sound like I have spies in there. I don't. But the castle has a lot of people who live and work there." Gran shrugged. "My friends and I know a few of them in passing."

Gran's friends were her buddies from the war. They were the finest soldiers the Kingdom of Midnight ever had. They were still all as fit as Gran and probably each had an armory as big as the one in this house.

"So that's why you weren't that curious about what happened to me. You know more than I do, don't you?"

"I want all the details, Ruby. But we don't have a lot of time. The hunters are likely to go out again soon before the moon wanes too much."

"I thought they only hunted on the full moon?"

"Usually. But they're getting desperate, I think. The king is not a patient man, and his demand for a pack of wolfkin is becoming intense."

"For what? Doesn't he have enough pets?"

"He's not as frivolous as people think he is. His cruelty and barbarism serve a purpose. He needs an army to protect his power."

"He has an army."

"An ordinary army isn't enough. We've already seen that."

"Are you really going to bring this back to your Wild Wars? I'm sorry the wars changed your life so much, but you have to move on, Gran. Not everything has to do with those ancient wars."

"I admit there's been a lull. But it's coming back strong now, just as all us soldiers knew it would."

"It's a phantom war, Gran. It's in your head."

"The king knows it's never been over, and that it's heating up again. That's why he's pushing his hunters and recruiting allies. He uses his full-moon hunts to strengthen ties and see who has the fortitude to withstand the coming days."

Ruby sat back, deflated. There were plenty of reasons to be paranoid in the Kingdom of Midnight. But the Wild Wars were not one of them.

Gran was too far gone in her delusion. Ruby wouldn't be able to help her. A crushing sadness came over her at the thought of her strong, capable grandmother being helplessly lost in the fog of old age.

"Oh, stop the moping before I smack it out of you, girl. If you won't believe your elders, I suppose I'll just have to convince you some other way."

Gran got up and walked out of the cottage. "Come on, Ruby. Do your best to keep up."

CHAPTER 29

*G*ran walked right into the forest.

Ruby hovered at the edge of the shadows. It was daylight, but the forest was still the last place she wanted to go to.

"Gran, where are you going?"

"Just follow me, and you should be all right." Gran didn't slow down.

Ruby hesitated. If she stood here any longer, she was going to lose Gran. Who knew what might happen to her in the woods?

She'd heard other people talking about their grandparents getting on in years and fading, but she never thought it would happen to her own Gran. She might be acting strange, but there was still nothing frail about her—far from it. She seemed more agile than ever.

Ruby couldn't see nor hear her now. She rushed after Gran. "Let's go back and finish our breakfast. I'll make you some tea."

"Stop treating me like an old woman, girl. My days are just beginning."

That was when Ruby noticed that Gran was walking through the forest barefoot.

"Don't you at least want to get your shoes, Gran?"

"Shoes make noise. I find this is stealthier."

"I'm sure it's more painful too."

"Oh, quit fussing like an old lady, Ruby. Stay quiet and follow me."

A lifetime of trusting Gran made Ruby follow her even into the deep forest.

After a while, Ruby began to step where Gran stepped, move as she moved. The small animals scurried about as though Ruby wasn't even there. It was remarkable how quietly Gran could move through the woods. She almost floated over the ground.

Ruby assumed Gran had knives hidden all over her. She never went anywhere without her weapons. But now that they were in the deep forest, Ruby wished she had armed herself beyond the knives that the hunters had given her.

She missed her bow and arrows. The hunters wouldn't let her have those, but she wished she'd thought about it before leaving the cottage.

Ruby didn't ask where they were going. If Gran wanted her to know, she would have told her. Besides, it was best to stay quiet in the woods.

Like before, Ruby quickly became lost. The more she thought about it, the more scared she got. It was daylight, but in the woods, they were always in deep shadow.

Gran had no hesitation in her steps. She was headed somewhere specific, and she seemed to know the way. Ruby certainly hoped that was the case.

After a while, they came to a clearing. Although the sky was visible, the clearing was so overgrown that it took Ruby a minute to realize that she was looking at a high wall. Brambles and creepers had covered the wall to the point of it being indistinguishable from the forest itself.

Gran didn't seem at all surprised to see this place. Before Ruby could catch her, she walked around the wall and stood in front of a gate.

The gate was high and ornate. But it was hard to see the original ornamentation because the creepers covered it so thickly.

Ruby might have walked right past this place without realizing what it was—a perimeter wall around an estate. She pushed the creepers aside and peered through the bars of the gate.

A pair of yellow eyes stared back at her from the other side. Large fangs dripped saliva from their tips.

Ruby yelped and jumped back, grabbing Gran and pulling her away.

"Open the gate," said Gran. "You're scaring my guest."

There was a low growl, but the gate opened enough to let Gran through.

"Gran!" Ruby tried to grab her arm, but her grandmother just shook it off.

"Maybe this will teach you to never doubt me. The next time you look at me like I'm senile, I swear I'll throw you to the wild fairies. Now, come on. Follow me."

The beast at the gate was a howler.

He was barefoot and bare-chested. There was no mistaking his savage wrongness. Like the creatures from the castle, he was hairy all over and his jaws were elongated enough to fit all those sharp teeth.

The beast growled at Ruby, looking like he wanted to eat her.

Gran growled back.

To Ruby's surprise, the creature backed away.

Ruby looked at Gran, then at the monster, then back at Gran.

"Come, Ruby. We have a lot to discuss."

The monster didn't attack. Instead, he closed the gate as though he was nothing but a gatekeeper. Unlike the shredded and filthy clothes she'd seen on the creatures at the castle, this one wore trousers made of fine material. They were intact and not even tattered above his bare feet.

When he saw Ruby looking at his clothes, he bared his teeth in a silent growl and snapped his fangs.

She scampered to Gran, who was walking ahead.

And that was when Ruby saw what they'd walked into.

It was a grand mansion sitting in a clearing surrounded by the dark forest. The grounds were manicured, with hedges shaped like animals and fountains dotting the garden. The nobles who lived here must be as wealthy as the king himself.

Gran walked along the path to the mansion with no hesitation. Ruby followed.

"Where are we?"

Gran just kept walking toward the front door. The front door, not the servants' entrance where she would normally enter to deliver flowers. Not that they had any flowers with them.

Gran walked through a matching set of large bushes shaped like giant wolf heads howling at the sky. They were placed on either side of the path so that Gran blocked her view as she walked through. Following her, Ruby walked past the giant topiaries.

The air exploded with snarls.

To her left, howlers jumped toward her. Their hairy faces were full of the twisted urge to attack like a wolfkin, even though they still had the arms and legs of a person.

There was a whole yard full of them.

Ruby pulled out her knives—one in each hand. Every muscle in her body was poised to fight almost before she knew what she was seeing.

The creatures reached out toward her in their mad intensity. Their stunted fingers were bloody, and their broken claws were full of dirt and flesh.

Their faces were full of fury, and all they seemed to want was to reach Ruby.

CHAPTER 30

*I*t took a moment before Ruby realized that the
howlers were chained.

Large chains crisscrossed their hairy chests and were
attached to their collars. They were leashed to pillars
embedded into the ground. It limited their range so that the
closest ones could almost reach the path, but not quite.

Ruby backed away toward the flower garden on the other
side of the pathway. Gran kept walking, not even looking
surprised at the monsters.

"Gran?"

"It's best to walk fast past them. You don't want to agitate
them too much."

It would be easier to just to go back the way they'd
come. But Gran didn't seem to have any intention of
leaving.

So Ruby raced past the gauntlet of twisted beasts to reach
her grandmother.

As she did, she noticed details that she hadn't seen before.
The creatures were chained, but whoever had chained them
had taken special care not to hurt them. The chains were

buffered by leather crisscrossing their chests so that it wouldn't dig into their skin.

The chains were linked to a leather collar, but the collar was loose. It looked like it was meant to keep the beasts from slipping out of the chains rather than to choke them. Each pillar had a bowl of water and a platter that was smeared with glistening blood. Raw meat—and recent, by the look of it.

Someone was caring for these beasts.

By the time Ruby made it through the gauntlet, Gran was already walking through a spectacular flower garden. Gran, being Gran, looked at the flowers with a professional eye.

It was an odd sight to see such delicate flowers growing next to a yard full of chained monsters. What kind of place was this?

Until now, Gran's flower garden was not only the best one Ruby had ever seen, it had been the only one. But this garden took Ruby's breath away.

There were flowers blooming here that Ruby had never imagined. They ranged from delicate pinks and violets to bold reds and purples. There were even blue and black roses tipped with yellow. Flowers of all shapes and sizes graced the grounds around the mansion.

The scent wafted to her. It was a wondrous scent that would make the richest noblewoman hunger to own it in a bottle.

"What is this place?" asked Ruby.

The front doors opened, and two intimidating men walked out. They stood at the top of the steps, looking more like dock workers than men who would come out of a graceful mansion. One was tall and broad and the other shorter and stout.

"I've brought her." Gran walked up the steps to meet them. "We don't have a lot of time, so talk fast."

The two men looked at Ruby with cold eyes, taking their time. Something about their look made her grip her knives harder.

"So this is Silver's granddaughter," said the stout man. "She looks scrawny and scared."

"Without her, you'll have no mission," said Gran. "So I'd be a little more polite, if I were you, Ketter."

Ruby frowned. Gran's voice had changed.

"Can she do this?" asked the tall man.

"Sure," said Gran in the voice that was not hers. "If she chooses to. Why don't you ask her, Lanson? She's right here." Gran gestured toward Ruby with a sarcastic smile.

Even the way Gran held her body had changed. She leaned against the stone balustrade with a careless attitude.

"You haven't told her you're not her grandma, have you?" asked Ketter.

"What?" Ruby stared at Ketter, then at Gran.

Gran shrugged. "It's a little awkward. People don't react well to being fooled...or finding out anything about..." She shrugged. "Anyway, I've been slipping in all kinds of hints and trying to let her know in other ways, but it's not an easy conversation."

"You're not my grandmother?" asked Ruby. She couldn't believe it. Yet she knew that something wasn't right.

"She works with us," said Lanson. "This is Briar. Let's just say that she has some unusual talents. She brought you here to see if we could help each other."

"Where is my grandmother?" Ruby gripped her knives but forced herself to keep them down.

"She's at Midnight Castle," said Lanson. "We're planning to get her out, and we could use your help."

"Why would she be at the castle? And why would you care?"

Ruby couldn't help but look at Gran—no, Briar. Gran was

right there…except that she wasn't. She looked like Gran, but she'd hopped onto the balustrade and was swinging her legs like a girl. It was hard to imagine Gran doing that.

"The king's hunters caught one of ours," said Lanson.

Ketter curled his lip and growled.

"He saved us by luring the hunters, but he was caught," said Lanson.

"What does that have to do with my grandmother?"

"A fortnight ago, your grandmother volunteered to be part of a small rescue team," said Lanson. "One was killed, one was injured, and your grandmother was captured."

A fortnight. She'd missed Gran by a fortnight.

"Why would she volunteer to go into the castle? Who are you people? Why would she risk her life to rescue this person?"

"She wanted to find you," said Briar. "She knew you were in the castle but couldn't find a way to get you out. When she found out that a rescue mission was being planned, she volunteered."

"No one in their right mind would say no to Silver if she volunteers to help on a mission," said Lanson.

"She survived, but got herself captured," said Briar.

"You make it sound like she had a choice," said Ruby, trying to ignore the odd feeling of talking to Gran about Gran.

Briar shrugged. "She really wanted to get you out of that horrible place. It wouldn't surprise me if she got captured just to see if she could free the two of you from the inside."

"That's what gave us this idea in the first place," said Lanson.

"What idea?" asked Ruby.

The men assessed her until she had to resist the urge to fidget.

"She's rather small for the job, don't you think?" asked

Ketter. "Who would believe that she could capture two wolfkin on her own?"

"So it's two now?" said Briar. "I thought you were planning on one."

"She's supposed to capture one, then two others will stalk her until the hunters find her. Then the *hunters* will capture the other."

"And the third?" asked Briar.

"He'll escape," said Lanson. "That should make it more realistic."

"So will killing a few hunters," growled Ketter.

"Briar tells us that you can bring wild wolfkin into Midnight Castle," said Lanson.

"Is this true?" asked Ketter. "Can you do it?"

"The hunters would capture any wolfkin they could get," said Ruby. "They'll take them to the castle. You don't need me."

"They'd take us to the castle in cages," Lanson growled. "We need someone to let us out."

"Us?" Ruby could no longer deny her suspicions about these people. Still, it took a moment to understand what he was telling her.

"Me and Ketter."

She looked closely at the men in front of her. They were not hairier than any of the village men. Their hair was neatly trimmed, and their nails clipped and ordinary. They were large and powerfully muscular, but nothing so unusual as to mark them as anything other than strong men.

"We are the kin of wolves," said Lanson.

Ruby stopped breathing for a moment.

She looked around at the mansion and its grounds. Aside from the chained monsters, she would have assumed this was a noble sanctuary in the forest. A mansion kept by a wealthy nobleman who wanted a country estate away from the court's madness.

Instead, Ruby realized that she was in the wolfkin's den.

CHAPTER 31

*R*uby stared at Lanson and Ketter, trying to make sense of what they were telling her.

"But you're...men," Ruby said.

"This is what a real wolfkin can do," said Lanson.

"We can shift completely between man and wolf," said Lanson. "But full wolfkin like us are becoming rare."

She remembered the wild wolfkin at the menagerie that the Huntsman had shown her. If what they were telling her was true, he must have been a man in wolf form.

"You know where our friend is being kept, don't you?" asked Ketter, eyeing her knowingly.

Ruby nodded. "I can tell you in detail how to find him on your own."

"Can you tell us in detail how to get out of those infernal cages on our own?" asked Lanson.

"They need someone to open their cages once they're in the castle," said Briar.

"Can't you do it?" asked Ruby. "You could disguise yourself as a guard or a hunter. That would be better than me trying to do it."

Briar shook her head sadly. "My talents don't work that way."

"She'll be busy helping us in other ways," said Lanson. "She'll reduce the guards at night and try to keep them from the cages. That'll give us time to get everyone out."

"You must have someone in the castle who can move freely about and can help," said Ruby.

"None who would risk getting anywhere near a wolfkin cage, much less open one," said Ketter. "We're known for having a bit of a temper."

"The hunters will trust you if you bring them a wolfkin," said Lanson. "They gave you knives to fight with. That takes trust. They won't guard you too closely if you come back to them voluntarily."

Now, Ruby understood.

"So you want me to get myself captured again, along with you, so that I can free you and your brethren."

They nodded.

"What about my grandmother? How will we find her?"

"Ah, that." Lanson took a deep breath. "Well—"

"She's in a wolfkin cage," said Ketter. "So, most likely, she'll be near us and you can let her out."

"Why would she be in a cage?" asked Ruby. It seemed to her that Gran would either be with the laborers or in the dungeon.

"Because your grandmother is a wolfkin," said Ketter.

Ruby could only stare at him. Her head was spinning in circles.

"*Temporarily*," said Lanson. "Ketter likes to be dramatic."

"It's not as dramatic as when she'll turn back into herself in a couple of days," said Ketter. "The Dark King will be fascinated when he hears that they've found a woman in the wolfkin cage. His damned sorcerers will be even more interested."

"What are you talking about?" Ruby could barely get the words out. "My grandmother is not a wolfkin."

Ruby remembered catching a glimpse of a silver wolfkin at the menagerie. She didn't get a good look, but now she wished she had. Had that been Gran?

"Silver is not a true wolfkin," said Lanson. "But she volunteered to be part of the first rescue mission. To keep up with the others, she managed to get a potion from a witch that changed her form into a large wolf for a few days."

"A *witch*? Gran doesn't deal with witches."

"Did she tell you she didn't deal with wolfkin, either?" asked Ketter. "And I suppose she told you that the Wild Wars were over? And that the Dark King farted flowers?" He snorted. "Who knew that Silver's granddaughter would be so naive?"

Lanson casually smacked Ketter on his chest with the back of his hand. "Enough."

"If you keep this up, Ketter, she might 'forget' to let you out of your cage when the time comes." Briar shrugged. "Might not be that big of a loss to the pack."

Ketter bared his teeth at Briar, but it was more for show than true aggression.

Ruby's grandmother had never actually said that she didn't deal with witches or wolfkin. She simply warned Ruby that they were deadly and to stay away from them. As for the Wild Wars, well, Gran had always talked about them as though they were still happening in the shadows.

"Is that why my grandmother was helping you?" asked Ruby. "Because you're all fighting in the Wild Wars?"

She held her breath. Perhaps one of the reasons why nobody in Ruby's generation believed that the Wild Wars were going on was that it was too much to handle. Daily life in the Kingdom of Midnight was hard enough. But if they were truly at war, that meant that life could end or erupt into an open massacre any day. It was too much to accept.

Lanson nodded. "Yes, Silver fights with us in the Wild Wars."

CHAPTER 32

"We need all the allies we can get," said Lanson. "The Wild Wars have simmered for a generation, but it's about to come to a boil. The last thing we need is our pack leader and our best operative both trapped in cages. Who knows what the Dark King's sorcerers are doing to them?"

Ketter growled and his eyes flashed yellow.

"Does the king know the Wild Wars are brewing again?" asked Ruby.

"We think so," said Lanson. "That's probably why he's pushing his hunters so hard to capture us for his army."

"He needs you," said Ruby. "Maybe—"

Ketter snorted. "The Dark King doesn't work with allies who are as strong as he is. He won't risk losing his power. He only works with groups that he can conquer and control. Everyone else is an enemy to be crushed."

"Silver volunteered to help because she wanted to get you out, and this was her chance," said Briar. "Now, you can help her."

"All you have to do is bring us to the hunters," said

Lanson. "And when they're all bedded down for the night, you open our cages. We'll do the rest."

"And if I don't agree?" asked Ruby. "All I have is your word as to what's happened. You tricked me and broke into my grandmother's house. And if you really are wolfkin, then I should run from you rather than help you. You almost ate me in the forest."

"We *helped* you in the forest," said Ketter. "You were like a kitten in the woods. You think you could have survived if we hadn't made it a point to keep you safe? I couldn't believe how many times you ran around in circles. You think it was a coincidence that you just happened to leave the forest where your grandmother's house was? We *guided* you there, and believe me, I would have much preferred to just leave your whiny, skinny, trembling little—"

"*Ketter.*" Lanson's voice took on a commanding tone, then it became gentle again when he looked at Ruby. "What he means to say is that Silver spoke very highly of you."

"And she would have our hides if we didn't protect you. So we did," said Ketter.

"You would be doing the right thing by helping us, Ruby," said Lanson. "The king and his sorcerers use dark magic on their captives in an attempt to control a wolfkin army. Everyone chained in this yard has been a victim of his experiments. They've been tortured body and soul, then ruined in their failed experiments."

Ruby didn't know if the chained beasts could hear them, but they began to howl. It was an unnatural noise that sounded like the howls of the damned.

"You're not just planning to free a couple of wolfkin, are you?" asked Ruby.

"We're also going to free as many howlers as we can," said Lanson.

"You're going to free them from their cages just to bring them here to be chained?" asked Ruby.

"It's temporary," said Lanson. "They're chained only to keep them from killing each other. We have a plan to help them."

"Does your plan include keeping them from killing villagers?"

"They *are* villagers," said Ketter. "These are *people*. They used to have families and ordinary lives until the Dark King got to them."

"Let me show you something," said Lanson. He walked down the steps and onto the path toward the chained beasts.

Ruby didn't have much of a choice, so she followed Lanson. He stepped off the path and took her along the edges of the grounds where the beasts were chained. They seemed less agitated with Lanson around than they were when she'd last walked past them.

Still, it was obvious that even Lanson wouldn't be able to control them all. Some were so agitated that they slammed against their chains repeatedly, trying to reach Ruby. Blood flowed down their chests along the leather straps that were clearly meant to protect them from the chafing of the chains.

Ruby wondered who managed to weave through the gauntlet of howlers to feed them. And why would anyone be so dedicated?

On the other side of the area of chained creatures were children. It was the oddest combination to see them side by side. The children looked poor in their patched clothes, but they looked well fed and cared for.

As if it wasn't odd enough that there was a children's yard beside the monsters' yard, several of the younger children were playing. Some had balls that they chased around. Some were chasing each other. And others were running around with chickens and chicks.

"Are these the servants' children?"

Ruby knew it was unlikely. She was sure that servants of a grand mansion such as this would have children who were better dressed. These looked like peasant children.

"These are the children of those men." Lanson pointed to the howlers chained to the poles.

"What?" Ruby stopped, watching a little girl get far too close to one of the howlers.

"This is the only way they can see their fathers."

The little girl held out her chick to the howler. The hairy monster growled and swiped his claws at her.

Ruby gasped, expecting to see the girl fly through the air with gashes on her face. Instead, she stepped back with empty hands.

The monster had swiped the chick out of the girl's hands and was stuffing it into his mouth. The yellow chick wiggled and squeaked all the way until the last feather disappeared into the howler's mouth.

The little girl stood back a few feet and watched.

"They won't hurt the little ones. The men are placed so that they can see their children walking among them. If any child was hurt, there would be severe retaliation by the father of that child, as well as by several of the others. They understand and don't harm any of the children."

"You use the children to feed the beasts?"

"The families choose to feed their loved ones. We don't force anyone."

Every chained howler had a platter and bowl of water beside him. Now, Ruby understood how they'd managed to do that.

"Couldn't you just chain them farther apart?"

"We could. But then they'd never have to fight against the unnatural instincts that the Dark King weaved into them. This way, they're reminded each day that they were once men—that they have children and family who they cared for. It keeps their connection to what they once were. We've had success with a couple of them. They eventually managed to control themselves enough for us to let them loose. The one who guards the gate, for instance."

Lanson continued to walk through the children's yard, and Ruby followed. Behind the mansion was a mini-village worth of activity. Women and older children washed laundry, hung sheets, and beat rugs.

"The king wants an army of wolfkin," said Lanson. "To do that, he needs to experiment. The howlers are as far as he's managed to get."

A large pig was roasting on a spit. A large vegetable garden was full of sprouting greens of various sizes and colors. People were going in and out of the back doors of the mansion, and Ruby guessed those were the kitchen doors.

"These are some of the families of those men," said Lanson. "Sometimes, we can find them, and sometimes, they'd rather pretend that their men are dead."

"What happens to the ones with no children to feed them?"

"Many of the children feed several howlers. The fathers don't like it and will sometimes thrash themselves against their chains so hard that we have to tend to their wounds. But overall, it works. The pack takes care of our own, even if it's not a peaceful process."

There was an odd tranquility here. Despite the howlers chained nearby, what she saw here would be considered by many in the Kingdom of Midnight to be serene and untroubled. No one bickered, and everyone seemed to be content to do their jobs.

There were even one or two who laughed. Ruby couldn't remember the last time she'd heard a laugh.

"Why are you showing me this?"

"I wanted you to see that we're not the monsters you think we are. That these men are more than just twisted creatures on a chain. There are lives and families at stake here. The Dark King is so obsessed with his war that he's willing to destroy our humanity. We can't let him."

Ruby thought about the Huntsman. Did he know that the Dark King used magic to twist people into monsters?

"We saved you, hoping that you would be worth saving," said Ketter as he walked up to them.

"And we hoped that you could help others who are also worth saving," said Lanson. "Will you help us free our brethren?"

Were they telling the truth?

As much as Ruby tried to convince herself that it was all lies, she couldn't help but believe it.

She thought about her grandmother being trapped in a cage. She remembered the howlers confined in the king's menagerie and saw them with new eyes.

But could she survive revisiting the castle?

Death might be the easier option compared to being a prisoner in Midnight Castle for the rest of her life.

Ruby nodded slowly. "Yes. I'll help you."

CHAPTER 33

*T*yler had never seen Shadow so puffed up with pride. His pet had never been a dominant dog, but strange things could happen when the natural order of the pack was disrupted by people.

The hunting dogs considered Tyler their alpha. Shadow, being Tyler's pet, was often an outsider even though he'd been born in the same litter as some of them. Today, though, Shadow was the lead working dog.

Tyler brought the pack to the barn where Ruby had slept. He let them sniff around while he looked for any scrap of cloth or item of clothing that might have her scent on it.

There was none. His men had done what they were expected to do—they didn't abuse her, but they didn't treat her like a guest. She had no extra clothes and there had been no pillows or blankets provided for her. She'd slept on the hay.

He grabbed a handful of hay to bring with him, but it wasn't the best option. The dogs would have to remember her scent through the ride into the forest, and then know to follow that scent among all the others when they were in the woods.

Shadow was the only one who might be able to track her. He had gotten distracted by the snake the last time, but who was to say that Ruby hadn't hid there for a time?

Tyler and his men loaded the dogs onto the wagons and drove into the forest. Behind the dogs were the wagons of war.

This was another of Tyler's ideas that his father had implemented. If ships could have cannons and ballistae mounted on them, why couldn't his wagons have arbalests mounted on them? The large crossbows were hard to manage. His men could only shoot two bolts during the time one of his hunters could shoot a dozen arrows.

The arbalests might be slow, but they were big and had a longer range than ordinary bows. The intent had always been to capture a wolfkin, not to kill them. But no matter what the Dark King wanted, self-defense came first as long as Tyler was in charge.

The wagons were of limited use in the forest, but everyone felt better having them than not.

He'd wanted to go back out last night, but the men he'd lost were fresh on his mind, and everyone was exhausted. He had to let his surviving men have a decent night's sleep before taking them back into the forest.

Even in daylight, though, he could feel the tension running strong with his hunters.

"We'll have hours before the sun sets." It was obvious, but Tyler wanted to reassure his men as best he could.

"The trail will be cold by now," said Clemens.

Clemens looked like he had a hangover, which was unlike him. Tyler had never known him to drink before a hunt. When Clemens did have a night out, though, his drinking partner had always been Mathewson.

"We'll either find Ruby or we won't," said Tyler. "If the trail leads to the wolfkin den, we'll be ready."

"And if it leads to a torn-up body?" asked Clemens.

Tyler paused only for a moment. "Then that's the end of it. We'll have to find another who is strong enough to survive being bait."

"They don't need to survive. They just need to be chewy enough for the beasts to take them back to their den, so we can track them."

Tyler rode toward the woods in silence.

At the edge of the forest, the sunlight seemed to stop as though refusing to enter the woods. As usual, a cool wind blew from the forest, like it was pushing away anyone foolish enough to want to come in.

"When I was a boy, the hunters used to hunt stag and boar in those woods with the king," said Clemens as they rode toward the shadow's edge.

"Another king, another lifetime," said Tyler.

"True. Times have changed. The stag in that forest probably have fangs now, and the boar can probably fly and kick your head right off."

"Have you been telling your granny's night tales to your sons again?"

"Grannies know these things. We used to make fun of her night tales when we grew to think of ourselves as men. Then the Dark King took the throne." Clemens nodded. "Grannies always know."

They rode through the shadow border into the forest where the light turned from overcast daylight to cool twilight. After that, all conversation died as every hunter tried to make as little noise as possible.

CHAPTER 34

The road through the forest became overgrown as they headed deeper into the woods. Having weapons mounted to the wagons was only good if they could bring the wagons with them. Tyler knew they'd have to leave the wagons, but he had hoped he could take them farther in than this.

He had taken a wrong turn. They could either backtrack or leave the wagons here as a base and go on horseback through the woods.

Tyler looked up at the sky. They had a few hours of daylight left, but if they turned around to find a better path, they'd likely end up wandering in the dark.

"We leave the wagons here. I want one man stationed at each wagon. When we come back, don't be spooked into shooting at us."

That was one of the first lessons of a hunter—shooting beasts and not hunters. But each year, there were accidents anyway.

Tyler took the dogs. Shadow took the lead. While the

other dogs were distracted and unsure of the scent, Shadow moved confidently.

At first, Tyler wasn't sure if Shadow knew where he was going. One of Tyler's greatest frustrations was not being able to speak the language of animals. It would make his livelihood a whole lot easier.

As soon as Shadow took them to the last location where they'd set their trap the other night, Tyler breathed a sigh of relief. His dog knew where he was going.

He felt even better when Shadow took them back to the same crevice in the rocks where he'd found the snake. Ruby must have hidden here after all.

There were so many men and dogs that they didn't even try to stay quiet. There was a dozen men and half as many dogs. Their numbers wouldn't be enough if they found a den of wolfkin filled with monsters, but Tyler hoped he had enough men and weapons to capture one or two.

That was the plan. Find where the wolfkin took the girl. Most likely, they'd eaten her in the forest. But they'd eaten their fill on the night of the attack. They could have dragged her to their den.

A small part of him hoped she was still alive somehow. But it had been two days. How often did wolfkin eat?

Even though he had a yard full of variations of them, Tyler didn't know how a wild wolfkin behaved. Even the one he'd captured didn't behave as expected. As the king's favorite pet, there was too much black magic being worked on him.

Shadow sniffed through the underbrush, moving steadily. Tyler and his men followed. Some were on foot while others were on horseback. The ones on foot were trackers. They were the best in the Kingdom of Midnight.

After going up and down, and even down a steep ravine,

Shadow suddenly stopped. He perked his ears. So did the other dogs.

There was a moment of silence among the animals. Then the dogs began to bark.

Their hackles rose, and many stood their ground, facing the same direction into the dim woods. A couple of the dogs even ran back to the hunters, whining in fear.

Shadow was the only one to run in the direction that the others were barking at.

Tyler spurred his horse to chase Shadow. As he rode, he reached for his arrow. He knew his men were doing the same. His hunters were all excellent bowmen. They could shoot blindfolded, riding backward if they needed to.

He hoped Shadow was smart enough to stay back if he found a wolfkin. Tyler raced between the trees, trying to see what the dogs were so excited over.

A patch of sunlight lit the woods ahead of him. Out of the foliage, Ruby stepped into the light.

Something strange happened to Tyler then. He felt a rush of wonder and shock.

Ruby's red hair glowed in the light. She didn't move like she was injured. There was no fresh blood on her.

She seemed to be all right. Better than all right. She looked like wonder itself to Tyler.

Shadow ran full force toward Ruby. Something was wrong. Shadow was snarling and barking.

Behind Ruby, a white wolfkin stepped into the light.

Tyler pulled his bow and aimed his arrow.

"Stop," said Ruby, holding her hand out.

Tyler almost couldn't stop. Anger and fear had gotten hold of him, and his hand wavered with indecision.

What finally got him to control his impulse to shoot was the realization that the wolfkin wasn't attacking Ruby.

His men held their arrows. They all knew that their

objective was to capture a wolfkin, not to save the girl. Everyone had assumed that Ruby was dead.

The surprise of seeing her alive had momentarily made Tyler forget the purpose of being out here.

His men, always quick to react, threw a net. It caught the wolfkin, but it also draped over Ruby.

Tyler jumped off his horse and raced toward her. He ran with his arrow aimed at the beast trapped in the net with Ruby.

One of his men shouted.

Two other wolfkin appeared on either side of Ruby. They came snarling and tense, ready to leap on the men.

The dogs were going crazy with their barking. They were as aggressive as Tyler had ever seen them. But Shadow was the only one who ran at the predators.

"No! Shadow!" Tyler yelled, but it was no use.

Shadow was about to be torn apart by not just one monster, but three.

Tyler shot his arrows. He got three off before Shadow reached the wolfkin.

There was a yelp among all the growling and barking. Men yelled. Nets flew through the air.

In all this chaos, the thing that caught Tyler's attention above all else was Ruby's scream.

CHAPTER 35

*R*uby clamped her mouth. Everything had been going as planned until the Huntsman shot Lanson.

Lanson was an enormous gray wolf. Bigger than an ordinary wolf, with knifelike teeth and claws, Lanson had a frightening essence. Too intelligent, too calculating, too hungry to be a natural animal.

But Lanson, in animal form or not, was still Lanson. And watching him be shot by the Huntsman, who didn't seem to realize he was shooting a man, was tragic in a way that Ruby couldn't comprehend.

Ketter, who was beneath the net with her, seemed to have changed his mind about the plan. His growl and fangs were freakishly fierce. He chewed at the net and leapt at the hunters as they neared.

Ruby worked to untangle herself from the net, trying to reach Lanson. But the net was fine and clung to her like a cobweb. Both she and Ketter were almost in knots by the time the hunters reached them.

Lanson lay on the ground, his four legs twitching. Three

arrows stuck out of him—two on his side and one in his shoulder.

Shadow was all teeth and fierceness, looking like he was ready to tear into Lanson.

"Shadow, no!" yelled Ruby.

That was a mistake. She was showing too much concern for the wolfkin.

It wasn't that she liked them so much—she hardly even knew them. But they were people with compassion for their own. And she had begun to think of them as fellow villagers.

The third wolfkin, whose name was Nate, was a huge black wolf with yellow eyes. He looked like a horrific nightmare come to life. He was supposed to be the one who escaped, while Lanson and Ketter were to go to Midnight Castle.

But instead of running, Nate chose to stay and defend Lanson. The hunters threw a net over both of them.

Ruby had seen men die before. She'd seen it as recently as a couple of days ago, when the wolfkin tore apart hunters. But there was something extra tragic about men killing men without even knowing it.

Many would not call wolfkin men, and she needed to think that way too, at least for now. It helped her play her part in this mad, mad scheme.

"Get this one first." The Huntsman pointed to Ketter, who kept yanking the net as he leapt to reach Lanson.

Ketter's paws were entangled in the net, but he didn't seem to care. He chewed on the net with his powerful jaws, tearing a hole through it.

The Huntsman slung his bow over his back as he walked to Ruby. A muscle in his jaw was twitching. He looked angry, but Ruby couldn't figure out if he was angry with her. Not that it mattered. But she couldn't help wondering.

He untangled her and pulled the net off her. As soon as he

did, she rushed to Lanson. She needed to look closely at his wounds. Maybe there was something she could do for him.

"What are you doing?" asked the Huntsman. "Have you gone mad? Getting close to an injured wolfkin is a death wish."

Lanson was twisting, trying to reach the arrows with his jaws. Blood pooled below him and soaked into the ground.

"Shh," whispered Ruby as she knelt by him. She petted his fur, feeling the warm blood that matted it.

All around her, everything quieted. Even the dogs stopped their barking.

Lanson put his head down and panted shallowly.

"Can you do something for him?" she asked the Huntsman.

He was staring at her in awed fascination. So were all the hunters, who'd stopped dragging the netted beasts. The wolfkin were quietly staring too.

"How are you touching a wolfkin without him tearing at you?" asked the Huntsman.

"I've...made friends with them," said Ruby. "Can you please help him?"

"We might if we can get near him," said the Huntsman. "Clemens has some field dressing experience. But it's not worth risking his life for an injured wolfkin. The king has no use for lame beasts."

Ruby looked around, trying to think of a convincing argument. She saw her answer in Ketter's frantic eyes.

"The other wolfkin will be more useful if they're not in a blood frenzy for revenge," she said. "I might be able to coax them into behaving a little if they saw you helping their pack mate. But if he dies in front of their eyes, they'll fight you to the death and take some of you with them."

Ketter growled, emphasizing her point. Nate took up the growl.

Even though Ruby had met Nate in human form, he still raised the small hairs on the back of her neck. He must have inspired the old stories of nightmare monsters coming in the dark to steal children.

The Huntsman took his bow from his back and nocked it with an arrow. The captured wolfkin growled and snarled, jerking against their nets.

There was a tense moment when Ruby was sure the Huntsman would shoot Lanson dead.

He looked at the wolf, then at her, then back again. The Huntsman nodded.

"If you can't control him, I'll shoot him the instant he gets aggressive," said the Huntsman.

Ruby nodded, gently stroking Lanson's head to try to calm him.

"Clemens," said the Huntsman, "see what you can do."

Clemens stepped forward and approached Lanson with due caution. He paused just out of striking distance of Lanson's claws.

Ruby watched Clemens, trying to see if he intended to exact revenge for the hunters that the wolfkin had killed. She could tell he was thinking about it. He obviously didn't want to save any of them.

He stepped forward with a grim expression and got down on his knees. He began to snap the arrows, leaving stubs large enough to grab but not so large as to catch on anything.

"Aren't you going to pull them out?" asked Ruby.

"The healer would have my head if I did that," said Clemens. "Only the shaft would come out and the arrowhead would be lost inside. The healer gets in a mighty temper when he has to fish around for an arrowhead."

Clemens wasn't gentle, but he was swift and didn't waste time. With Ruby's help, he stanched the blood around the embedded arrows as quickly as possible.

CHAPTER 36

*T*yler couldn't believe his luck. Ruby was alive. And they'd captured three wolfkin.

His mind reeled at what he'd witnessed. Ruby had befriended the wolfkin. How was that possible?

He watched her sitting in the wagon ahead of him as it jounced along the path. The wolfkin were stowed in the cage wagon ahead of her. The horses pulling that cart were mad with fear and raced as fast as they could. If it took too long to reach the castle, Tyler would have to replace those horses before they collapsed.

Ruby had asked to be in the cage with the injured beast, but Tyler wouldn't allow that.

Tyler had never captured more than one beast before, so the issue of putting the wolfkin all in the same cage had never come up. He would have preferred to separate the injured wolfkin from the others, but he only had one cage wagon. And he'd merely brought that in a fit of optimism, not truly expecting to capture any.

Injured or not, Tyler wasn't about to leave a wolfkin out of a cage. He didn't think it had much of a chance of survival, especially with the others in the cage. He wondered if they would eat their own, now that one was weak.

They did not. He couldn't be sure, but it was possible that they did just the opposite. The wolfkin lay with their paws over each other in a way that just happened to put pressure around the injured one's wounds, stanching the blood flow. The cage was too small for the three of them, so they had to lie on top of each other, but he wondered if it was simply coincidence.

Tyler looked at Shadow as he sat on the wagon with Ruby. Shadow normally trotted along beside Tyler. Instead, he lay with his head on Ruby's lap.

All the animals were acting strange. Was Ruby some kind of beast whisperer? Did she befriend every creature that attacked her?

Tyler had never heard of such a thing. Perhaps she had some wild magic in her. That would explain why he was becoming so fascinated with her.

The men were silent as they rode through the woods. They might have captured three wolfkin, but that didn't mean there weren't more tracking them. The only way a hunter survived was to respect the power of the forest and its creatures.

His hunters were spooked. Tyler could feel the tension. What happened today wasn't just luck. Something strange was happening, and all his men could sense it.

If it was up to Tyler or any of his hunters, they'd simply leave the monsters here and run as far as they could. The men would probably let Ruby go too. Nobody wanted anything to do with monsters if they could help it.

But the Dark King wanted his wolfkin more than Tyler had ever seen him want anything. The longer it took to catch one, the more the king pressured him. Tyler was sure that soon, the king would begin to torture and execute the hunters one by one in front of the others. That was his usual method of motivation.

By the time they reached the castle, it was the middle of the night. Tyler gathered his thoughts. He'd have to report to the king as soon as they returned.

He'd dreamt of this moment when he could tell the king that he'd captured a wolfkin. He'd only managed to do it once, and he had to admit that had been an unforgettable moment. The king had smiled and seemed genuinely thrilled.

Of course, Tyler's father had also captured a wolfkin, and no doubt the king had been pleased. That hadn't lasted long, though.

Tonight, Tyler would be able to tell the king that he'd captured three wolfkin. He should feel elated and triumphant. Instead, he felt confused.

There was something wrong here. His instincts were warning him to stay far away from what was happening, if he didn't want to end up like his father. But he had no choice. So he would have to tread very carefully.

The big question looming in Tyler's mind was whether to tell the king of Ruby's involvement. He could simply mention that the girl survived by some miracle. Or he could take the other path and go into detail about her not having any fear of the wolfkin.

They hadn't attacked her, even when she was caught in the net with one of them.

When he closed his eyes, he couldn't get the image of her standing in the sun with that white wolfkin beside her. The beast didn't look like he was stalking her at all. He looked like he was walking beside her.

If the Dark King found out about Ruby, she would attract his fascination. In Tyler's opinion, it was never good to gain the king's attention. Even the nobles who fawned over him looked uncomfortable the minute the Dark King looked at them.

Tyler was sure the king would test Ruby by throwing her into a cage with a wolfkin. Tyler's chest tightened when he thought of that.

Still, if the king ever found out that Tyler had kept such an important piece of information from him... Tyler didn't want to think about that, either. He had his father to take care of, as well as his heritage of holding the position of the Royal Huntsman. It was an honor that had been passed down from father to son for generations.

Aside from that, he had his own life to protect. It was ridiculous to even consider risking it for this girl. She wasn't even an ordinary village girl. She was the property of the Dark King.

Tyler dismounted his horse in the middle of the castle courtyard. He let his men handle the details of settling in the beasts as he walked into the castle.

He took a deep breath and headed for the Dark King's chambers.

CHAPTER 37

*R*uby wasn't allowed in the cage with Lanson. It wasn't what the wolfkin would want anyway. He'd want her to concentrate on getting the key and setting them free.

That was beyond difficult. For one thing, the wolfkin had no specific plan for her to follow. They'd left it up to her to figure it out. They didn't know the layout of the wolfkin yard or the routines of the hunters. Only she knew that.

She wasn't sure if she should be proud that they relied on her or be anxious that their plan hinged on her doing her part.

When they reached the castle, the Huntsman got off his horse and walked into the castle without a backward glance.

"Every woman looks at our Huntsman that way," said one of the hunters. "I've never understood why women like pretty men. A true man has broken teeth and wears the clothes that have been good to him every day for years."

He smiled at Ruby, showing his broken teeth.

Ruby hopped off the wagon with Shadow following her. She expected to go back to the barn where she'd always slept.

She wasn't sure where that was from here, considering she'd never been in this courtyard. They'd left from a different area the last time she was in the castle.

But the hunters and their assistants were so preoccupied with the captured wolfkin that everyone seemed to have forgotten about her. She stood by the wagon, trying to blend in. She watched the men carefully to see who had the keys to the cage.

As she watched, she realized something that stunned her. The cages had no locks on them. The latch was a multi-step mechanism that animals couldn't work. A smart creature might be able to figure it out, but they wouldn't have the dexterity to work the latch.

She wouldn't need to get a key. All she'd need to do was sneak over to their cages at night and set them free. It would be surprisingly easy.

Ruby had to work to hide her elation and keep a straight face.

Once the hunters were off their horse, the entire group of men and the cage wagon rolled through the courtyard and to the back. Ruby, not knowing what to do, followed.

After a while, she recognized where they were. They were heading toward the menagerie. It was just outside the castle wall, not too far from the edge of the forest. The yard where they held their beasts and wild wolfkin sprawled along the rocky slope of the hill. Ruby guessed that the Dark King wanted enough space to grow when he had amassed an army of beasts.

When they reached the yard, a boy fetched a man who was still in his nightshirt. The man carried a leather bag that looked heavy. Ruby assumed this was the animal healer, but he wouldn't get anywhere near the wolfkin cage.

The two uninjured wolfkin were on their feet, growling

at the people around them. Their hackles were up, and they looked ready to tear apart anyone who came within range.

"Whose idea was it to put them all in the same cage?" the healer asked irritably. "How do you expect me to reach the injured one?"

The wolfkin bared their fangs and leapt at the cage bars, daring anyone to come near. They were so large that the three of them barely fit in that cage. But they managed to slither gracefully past each other without stepping on Lanson.

"Don't you have anything that will put them all to sleep?" asked Clemens.

"I can put a lamb to sleep, or a dog," said the healer. "But a wolfkin? I'd have to guess how much to give them and have no way of making sure that each eat the proper portion. It could kill them if I give too much, and then the king will kill me."

"I'll distract them to the back of the cage," said Ruby. "You can pull the injured one out."

The healer looked at her as if she was insane. But the men just looked uncomfortable. One even took a step away from her.

"Who is this?" asked the healer.

"Do you want to keep your head, or would you rather let the Dark King kick it around like a ball?" asked Ruby. "Pull out the injured one while I distract the others."

Ruby ignored the healer's stare and walked to the front of the cage wagon. The wolfkin were so fearsome that she didn't want to get too close. She wasn't sure how much of the man was still there when he was in wolf form.

She couldn't count on them thinking and behaving like the men she'd met. So she didn't touch the bars, but she got as close as she dared.

"Let them take him," she whispered. She knew the others

were listening, so even in her soft whisper, she didn't call Lanson by name.

The wolfkin continued their snarling at the men, every muscle in their enormous bodies tense.

"Shh," said Ruby. "Come growl at me if you must. But you need to let the men take your friend. He'll bleed to death if you don't."

The wolfkin ignored her and snarled even louder. They leapt on the cage bars, rattling the entire wagon and threatening to tip it.

Ruby didn't know what to do. Had they turned fully wolf? Could they no longer understand the language of people?

Out of desperation, she began to hum a lullaby that Gran used to sing to her. The jumping and crashing of their bodies against the bars quieted a little, so she continued.

She hummed louder and as melodically as she could. Gradually, the wolfkin calmed down. Until finally, the two wolfkin turned away from the men and both leaned against the front of the cage where Ruby stood.

The entire yard seemed to quiet, as though even the howlers were listening to Ruby's humming.

She made sure not to interrupt the humming as she motioned for the hunters to get Lanson out of the cage. The men hesitated, each clearly not wanting to be the one to open the cage.

Then one of the men stepped forward and paused by the cage door. Two others stepped behind him. The remaining men nocked their arrows and aimed at the wolfkin.

Ruby almost stopped her humming when she saw the arrows. But she kept the music going. Either the wolfkin really were entranced by the music, or the men within the beasts had managed to gain control.

The hunters looked nervous. It was clear that everyone

feared the wolfkin. It was also clear that no one wanted to be the one to kill one of the king's precious wild pets.

The man in front of the cage door took two large breaths, then opened the cage.

Ruby hummed louder, moving her hands in front of the wolfkin to keep them distracted.

The men reached in and dragged out Lanson as quickly as they could. The two wolfkin in front of Ruby twitched and snarled. Ruby could tell they knew what was happening and that they were fighting their instincts.

She hummed with all the intention and emotion of telling them how important it was that they control their animal side. Lanson's life depended on it.

Then it was over. The men shut the cage door.

As soon as the metal door clanged against the cage, the two wolfkin spun and roared. It was a sound that struck at the heart of primal fear—a sound no creature was meant to hear and live to tell of it.

The wolfkin slammed against the cage door, rattling the entire wagon.

"I'll go with them," Ruby said into the cage. "I'll do what I can to keep him safe."

Ruby ran after the men who were hoisting the injured wolfkin onto a stretcher. She talked nonsense to Lanson—half humming and half speaking—as she stood by. She continued her reassuring chatter as the men dragged the stretcher through the yard.

CHAPTER 38

*T*yler watched at the edge of the menagerie as his men opened the cage. He had his bow ready with an arrow nocked, aimed at the wolfkin.

He didn't need to be close to hit a target and hadn't had time to intervene. His mistake was that he hesitated when he first came onto the scene. Ruby's humming had charmed the beasts and watching that happen had mesmerized Tyler.

If he had personally overseen the settling in of the wolfkin, this wouldn't have happened. He didn't know what he would have done, but it wouldn't have been this. Letting one of the monsters die was preferable to letting half of his men die and setting loose two wolfkin so close to the castle and village.

The king would not have agreed. And Tyler's men knew that. But the king didn't have to face the families of dead men, nor would he be haunted by them in his sleep.

Tyler held his breath like an amateur. When he realized what he was doing, he forced himself to breathe again. A hunter wouldn't last long if he held his breath every time he needed to shoot.

The girl, though... He could hardly comprehend what was happening. He could hear her humming. Beautiful and ethereal. It promised the kind of comfort and love that he hadn't felt since his mother was alive and he could barely walk.

He couldn't believe what he was seeing. The monsters were entranced by her. While the beasts were distracted, his men managed to drag the injured wolfkin out of the cage.

When the cage door slammed shut, Ruby began to talk to the wolfkin in her soft voice. Tyler couldn't make out her words, but he could hear her tone. Soft. Reassuring. Full of promises.

Tyler lowered his bow and put away his arrow, never taking his eyes off her. When she was done talking to the beasts, she rushed over to the injured wolfkin.

Tyler walked the rest of the way into the yard and took a good look at the monsters in the cage. They were huge and full of fury again now that Ruby had left. The wagon rocked back and forth as they slammed themselves against the bars.

Tyler tried something, just out of curiosity. He tried talking to them the way he would to his men if they saw one of their own being dragged away.

"We'll do our best to keep your friend alive."

The wolfkin snarled at him, clawing through the bars.

Tyler looked at Ruby. She was crooning to the injured wolfkin as they dragged him to the healer's quarters. Could she really befriend and manage these monsters?

The king would be very keen to meet her.

Tyler had gone into the king's chambers with every intent to include Ruby in his report. But it hadn't happened that way.

He couldn't say why, but by the time he left the Dark King's chambers, he'd only briefly mentioned that they'd discovered the wolfkin with the girl they'd used as bait. He left the king with the impression that Tyler's trap had worked after all.

He could be executed for keeping an important piece of information from the king. But in the back of his mind, he'd come up with excuses that might sound legitimate. He didn't know for sure that Ruby could manage the beasts, and the king was too busy to be bothered with theories.

Still, Tyler should have told the details of what had happened—how the wolfkin hadn't attacked her, how she was whole and uninjured.

Tyler followed his men to Magnus's cottage at the edge of the yard. Magnus and his family had lived and worked there for generations as the castle's animal healer. It used to be a tranquil place, where injured dogs and sheep were taken to be healed. These days, it was a nightmare position that required any sane man to drink lots of wine just so he could sleep at night.

Tyler's feet crunched the gravel on the way to the healer's cottage. The injured wolfkin must be in bad shape because he wasn't snarling. None of the men were talking, either, although a few of them were making the sign of the old religion, even though the Dark King had outlawed it.

Most of Tyler's men stood outside the cottage, clustered together like a band of boys.

"Go put the new wolfkin near the other ones," said Tyler. "There's less to agitate them there. Oh, and make sure to feed and water all of them. And if any of you mistreats any of the beasts, there's nothing we can do to keep the Dark King from feeding you to his new pets. Understood?"

His men nodded with grim expressions and went to work. Tyler usually didn't need to remind them of their duties, but with the death of their friends so fresh in their hearts, he needed to make sure they understood what was at stake.

Tyler walked into Magnus's cottage. Inside, the air was warm with the body heat of so many in such a small space. The smell of blood and fear permeated the place. Beneath that were the acrid scents of animal piss and alcohol.

Tyler took a good look at Magnus to see if he was sober. They'd grown up together, both knowing that they'd follow in their fathers' footsteps even as children. They'd each had to take over their fathers' positions years before they should have.

Magnus looked like he was following his father's footsteps a little too closely. Wine, stress, and lack of sleep had killed Magnus's father, and Magnus was beginning to look far too much like him. Even though he was a couple of seasons younger than Tyler, he looked twenty years older.

If it had been another time, with another king, Magnus would have been a content man working with hunting dogs and farm animals.

The healer didn't look quite sober, but his hands were steady as he pulled out the arrows. The wolfkin lay on the table with a metal muzzle on him and his legs tied with rope.

Two of the arrows came out without their arrowheads. Magnus did his best to shave the area and dig around to pull them out. Four men held down the wolfkin while he worked.

When Magnus was done taking out the arrowheads, Clemens approached with a searing rod straight out of the fire. He'd volunteered to cauterize the wounds. Tyler was sure it was a job the others envied.

The cottage filled with the scent of burning flesh and fur as Clemens pressed the red-hot metal on the wound. The look on Clemens's face was vicious pleasure as the wolfkin cried out and thrashed in pain. Clemens didn't press so hard as to do more harm than necessary, but he did seem to keep the hot rod on the burning skin longer than he needed to.

The other men practically growled their approval. The

wolfkin jerked and emitted a tortured sound that was part yelp and part growl.

Howls erupted outside.

All through the menagerie, howls filled the air. The beasts who were created by dark magic made an unnatural tortured howl that matched their unnatural tortured bodies. The sound was full of madness and suffering.

Ruby seemed oblivious to all of it. She was concentrating on whispering to the injured wolfkin. Beads of sweat moistened her brow as she tried to soothe the creature.

Tyler didn't know if her nonsensical words soothed the wolfkin, but he guessed that his men would have a much harder time controlling the beast without Ruby. She seemed to have a way of bringing out a gentler side of killer dogs and monsters alike.

A tiny spark of hope flared in Tyler as he watched her work. He refused to let it grow, but he couldn't extinguish it either.

On the second cauterization, the wolfkin went limp.

"Is it dead?" asked Clemens. He pulled back his metal rod, holding the red-hot end in the air above the limp body.

Magnus felt the beast's throat. "Not yet." Then he took the opportunity to rub salve over the cauterized wounds while the wolfkin lay still.

"You're going to be all right," whispered Ruby beside the limp beast. "You're as strong as can be. And you don't want to die because of three little splinters, do you?"

Tyler almost smiled at that. No one had called his deadly arrows splinters before.

"Girl, come with me," said Tyler.

Ruby stood up, looking at him with surprise. Had she thought that she had been forgotten? Did she truly believe a woman like her could be forgotten?

Tyler motioned for her to leave the cottage ahead of him. She obeyed.

He called himself all kinds of fool for getting his hopes up. But he couldn't help it. It seemed the king and this infernal kingdom hadn't smashed all hope out of him after all.

If she could soothe a creature like this, could she soothe his father as well?

CHAPTER 39

Tyler had planned to take Ruby directly to his father, but Shadow followed them. He could have ordered the dog to stay, but Shadow always kept Tyler company on the path to his father.

So he indulged his dog yet again. Tyler walked Ruby and Shadow to the kitchen, where he got his usual bone for his dog to keep him occupied outside his father's fence.

Tyler had to admit that perhaps it wasn't all about spoiling Shadow. There was something nice about walking with Ruby, and he wanted to take the long route by going to the kitchen first. She was mysterious to him in so many ways.

Question after question bubbled in him that he wanted to ask her. But he was tired beyond belief. He hadn't slept much last night and not at all the night before.

He'd been on high alert for days, trying to keep his men alive both during the hunts and with the Dark King. One misstep and his entire world could crumble. There was no doubt that the Dark King was as dangerous as walking into a wolfkin den.

And then there was the girl. There was no reason why Tyler should worry over her. Certainly, she was the best candidate to be a lure for the wolfkin, but his concern went beyond that. And that made him cautious.

The last thing he needed was to be sweet on a girl whom the Dark King might take an interest in. Catching the king's interest was worse than being bait.

The kitchen was warm and full of comforts, as usual. The smell of bread always wafted there. The kitchen maids were shyly kind to Tyler and always asked about Shadow. He knew he could have any of the kitchen maids if he wished, but he liked the comfortable welcome he'd received all his life here. The last thing he wanted was to spoil it with an awkward tryst.

It was here that he'd gotten his scrapes cleaned and bandaged when he was a boy. Here where he'd had warm late-night meals after a hunt. Here where his mother used to work as cook before the pox got to her.

He also liked showing Ruby that he wasn't a monster. That women were not afraid of him and, in fact, welcomed him. The older cooks who'd known him since he was a child chatted with him while the younger kitchen maids shyly smiled at him.

They all looked at Ruby with curiosity. He didn't bother to introduce her to anyone, though. That would be worse than naming an animal destined for slaughter.

Perhaps he could make a rule for himself that after the third time he took her to visit the kitchen with him, he could introduce her...

Tyler shook his head. There wouldn't be a second time, much less a third.

He collected Shadow's bone and said a quick farewell as they left. Ruby looked at him differently when they got out of the kitchen.

"They seem nice," she said.

"They are. That's usually the best place in the castle to visit, unless the king is having a feast or asking for special dishes."

"They don't like making special dishes?"

"They find it distressing. The king is very particular about how his enemies are cooked."

"Oh."

That shut down her questions. Tyler was too tired for interrogations or politics or ethics. He needed all his energy for the visit to his father.

"Talk to me about your life," he said. "What did you do at home?"

She looked surprised at his question, but dutifully answered. "I helped my grandmother grow flowers and sell them at the market."

"Flowers? Is this the same grandmother who taught you how to fight?"

"The very one. She has many talents and interests."

"I can see that. Did she raise you?"

"Practically. My mother died when I was young. I live with my father, but it was Gran who raised me."

"My mother died when I was young as well, but it was my father who raised me. It was a very manly household."

"I imagine it was. He taught you how to shoot?"

He nodded. "He was the king's Huntsman."

"You're an excellent bowman. I've never seen anyone shoot that fast or with that much accuracy."

"My father taught me everything I know. He started my training as soon as I could walk."

"So did my grandmother." She must have forgotten that she was in Midnight Castle for a moment because she smiled.

Tyler was mesmerized by that smile.

There was magic in the sound of the frogs and the crickets as they walked through the empty courtyard toward the animal pens. It was unusually warm this night, warm enough for fireflies to come out, lighting the courtyard like blinking stars.

"Was he a good father?" she asked. "I've heard that being near the king causes people to twist in dark ways."

"He was a good father." Tyler didn't elaborate on how the king *had* caused his father to twist in dark ways.

They walked through the kennels. He swore Shadow puffed up when he walked through the kennels beside Tyler while the other dogs watched from their pens.

"Shadow seems happy with you," she said.

"He was until he found you. You must have some kind of magic over animals."

"It wasn't magic. Just bribery. Shadow is surprisingly easy to bribe."

"Yes, the main reason he's happy to be with me right now is because he knows he's about to get this bone." Tyler had gotten an especially meaty joint this time, and Shadow was literally drooling for it.

"But I wasn't just talking about your uncanny ability to befriend dogs," he said.

Ruby's expression turned cautious. He regretted that, so he let it go for now. There would be plenty of time for inter-rogation in the morning when he'd had a decent night of sleep.

Tyler dropped the bone at the fence separating his father's yard from the rest. Shadow plopped down and began happily gnawing.

Tyler braced himself as he led the girl into his father's yard.

CHAPTER 40

$\mathcal{T}$yler watched Ruby as she stared at his father in the cage. She'd fought and even killed someone like his father.

Father's mouth was so full of fangs that he couldn't close his lips. His snout was long and black, while the rest of his face was mottled. He was hairy, like the rest of his kind, but he had a stubby tail which many of them did not.

Standing like a man, he tried to grip the bars of his cage. His hands were paw-like, with stunted protrusions that used to be fingers. He had nails that were thicker than a man's but not so thick as a wolf's claws.

His nails were splintered and broken. Two of them were actually ripped all the way to the edge, looking like they'd been pulled out.

There was nothing that Tyler could do about any of it. He couldn't so much as put a bandage on his father's ripped-out fingernails. Those fingers had been all right yesterday, and no one who worked for him would dare harm his father.

So that meant that his father had pulled out his own fingernails. He was getting more agitated and aggressive every day. One of these days, Tyler was going to have to admit that the father he knew was gone.

But not yet. Not tonight.

Tonight, he had a tiny flame of hope.

Father howled when he saw Ruby. It was a pitiful sound, but it probably struck fear into everyone else, except Tyler. Well, perhaps Ruby recognized the sound as sad rather than frightening too.

She must have thought that it was an odd sort of place. The cage was larger than the others, and half of it had a roof to shelter against the rain.

There was a bench that sat near the cage—not so close as to be dangerous, but closer than any normal person would want to be. The yard wasn't bare ground like the rest of the menagerie. There were plants and even a small pond with frogs hopping in it.

Ruby glanced at Tyler. He could tell she was wondering if this was another test. Did she think that he wanted her to fight this creature?

"Will you talk to him the way you did to the wild wolfkin?" asked Tyler.

She looked at his father in the cage. Father reached through the cage bars, trying to get at her. Many of the other cages had bars that were close enough to keep their arms from going through. But this one had wider space between the bars.

"What do you want me to say?" she asked.

"Whatever it is you say to these creatures."

"For what purpose?"

"To soothe him."

"That's it?"

"For now."

"Why?"

"What does it matter?" he asked. "Just do it. Please."

Ruby looked surprised, and he realized that it was because he was pleading with her. She was a prisoner as much as any of the howlers, and he was her captor.

She looked unsure if she could soothe his father. He found that odd, since she'd managed to calm wild-caught wolfkin. Wouldn't this be much easier?

Of course, there was the taint of black magic that the Dark King had used to torture and turn his father. There was no accounting for that.

She cleared her throat nervously. Then she began to hum the same lullaby that she'd sung to the wolfkin.

Tyler watched his father as she hummed.

Father howled—a pitiful sound full of pain and anguish. If anything, he seemed to become more agitated. He banged against the cage.

Ruby continued her humming, trying to sound soothing. It must be hard to hum when what she really wanted to do was run from Father's rage.

"Enough." Tyler couldn't keep the disappointment out of his voice.

She watched him carefully, her hand inching to her knife at her waist. She must have assumed that he was testing her somehow, and that she'd failed.

He considered taking away her knives, but if she wanted to stick him with it, she'd had plenty of chances to do it. Right now, he didn't care much about it.

"Are you all right?" she asked.

Tyler almost laughed. It was ridiculous to ask about his well-being when he was her captor. But she seemed reluctantly concerned. He nodded.

"What do you intend to do with the wolfkin?" she asked.

"Whatever the king wants me to do."

He watched his father in the cage as he settled down. Apparently, the beast in him hadn't liked Ruby's lullaby.

Perhaps it only reminded him of the human life that he could no longer have. There was so much anguish and loss in his howling.

"Why didn't your song have the same effect on him as it did on the wolfkin?"

"This isn't a wild wolfkin."

"Neither is Shadow."

"Both Shadow and the wolfkin are as nature intended," she said. "I've heard that the howlers are forged with black magic. Is it true?"

Tyler swallowed the old anger that boiled up whenever he thought about it.

"Do you..." She chewed her lip. "Is this howler...special?"

If he didn't know better, he'd think that she knew the king's howlers were often made from ordinary people. But she couldn't know that. Anyone who talked about that would be killed for treasonous gossip.

"Why did you come back?" he asked.

"I didn't. You and your hunters found me."

"Alive. How was that possible?"

"I don't know." She gave him a small smile. "Maybe the wolfkin just needed a woman's touch."

He frowned. He didn't like that answer. He thought about why as he watched his father in the cage.

Father watched him back and snarled at him. There was no doubt in Tyler's mind that, if given the chance, his father would eat him.

At times like this, it was Tyler who wanted to howl.

CHAPTER 41

There was something deeper going on in this private garden than what the Huntsman was telling Ruby. She felt the deep care and tenderness that went into every detail here.

She felt the tug to help ease whatever was weighing on the Huntsman. Ruby could almost hear Gran scoffing at that. *There is no room for a young girl's fancy during a war,* she'd say.

Gran had been a young girl during the Wild Wars. Had she ever felt torn between duty and compassion?

Ruby sighed. Gran was right. There wasn't a lot of time to spend on whatever the Huntsman was going through. Lives were at stake, and it was up to her to figure out how to free the wolfkin.

There was an opportunity here. She needed to think about how to convince the Huntsman to give her the freedom to do her part of the mission.

"Perhaps I should stay the night with the injured wolfkin back at the healer's cottage?" asked Ruby.

The Huntsman tore his gaze away from the beast in the cage. He had gone somewhere deep inside—somewhere sad, she could tell. It tugged at her heart and she didn't like that.

He was her enemy. He was the enemy of everyone she was working with. She didn't want to see this side of him.

Was this howler someone who had been the Huntsman's family member? A brother or father?

"Why?" he asked.

"I may be useful to the healer if I stay there for the night."

Ruby held her breath as he thought about it but tried to look as if it would be a mere favor to him.

"There's nothing more dangerous than a wounded beast," he said.

"That's why he may need my help. The injured wolfkin will be calmer if he sees me, I'm sure of it. I'll stay out of the way if I'm not needed."

"Why would you do this?"

Ruby shrugged, trying to look casual. "I'm your prisoner again. I'd rather you think of me as someone useful beyond just being bait."

He frowned at her. Did she say something wrong?

"All right. You can stay the night at the healer's cottage."

Ruby couldn't believe it. It was that easy. The healer's cottage wasn't meant to keep people in. All she had to do was sneak out in the middle of the night and open the wolfkin cages.

She schooled her face. She'd slipped up. She could tell by the keen look in the Huntsman's face that he saw the brief elation pass through her.

He gestured for her to leave the fenced garden. Now that the beast in the cage had calmed down, she was reluctant to go. It was a peaceful area. The frogs began to croak again, and dragonflies flew lazily over the pond.

Shadow was happily gnawing on the bone just outside the fence. The Huntsman picked it up right out of the dog's jaws, and Shadow let him. They must have had a close relationship for such a large dog to allow that.

Shadow looked up at the Huntsman with adoration. He showed no signs of being even the slightest bit afraid of the man. Ruby trusted Shadow's instincts. If this was a man that Shadow could love, then he must have earned it somehow.

That worried her. Not wanting your enemy to be killed or seriously hurt was a problem during a war.

This isn't a war.

And if it was, it wasn't *her* war. It was Gran's and the wolfkin's...

Ruby sighed. She supposed that it was her war now too.

"Does your family live here?" she asked. She wanted to distract herself from her thoughts, but now that she'd asked the question, she became curious.

"Yes." He didn't sound happy about it, nor did he invite further questions.

Their boots crunched for a while as they walked. Then, as though he was trying to distract his own thoughts, he asked, "And you? Where is your family?"

"They're in the village. We're nothing special. We sell things at the market, tend to our garden, and live a quiet life, mostly."

She hoped he wouldn't ask for further details. She realized that chatting with the Dark King's huntsman could be more dangerous than her own thoughts.

"I usually don't get tongue-tied around a girl. You have a rather odd effect on me, Ruby."

She misstepped in her surprise. "What?"

He slowly began to smile when he looked at her. "You haven't had many suitors, have you?"

"Suitors?" She felt heat rising to her cheeks. "What's that? Do you mean hunters chasing me down like a rabbit in the woods? Or wolfkin scaring the living daylights out of me? If that's what you mean, then I suppose I've had more than my fair share."

"Life is difficult for everyone in Midnight. But surely a woman like you must have suitors vying to protect your honor. Where is that cur? How has he managed to let you be a captive in Midnight Castle?"

"My grandmother says girls should always be selective and never feel rushed."

"Your grandmother is a wise woman. So have you selected someone?"

Ruby thought about the boys she'd known in the village. None of them interested her. The ones she found the most interesting were the ones all the village girls were interested in. Usually, they were men from outside their village. There were even guards from the castle that some girls admired, but Ruby couldn't imagine life with someone like that.

"For me, I think it would have to be someone from outside the village. Someone exotic but stable."

"Usually, the word 'exotic' goes with danger."

"That's the last thing I want. I've had enough danger to last me a lifetime."

"Me too."

"You're not married?"

"No. I've watched too many hunter wives turn into widows to want that for myself."

"So you'll never get married?"

"I didn't say that. It's not impossible that I'll find another hunter."

Ruby frowned. "Does the Dark King have women hunters?"

"There are none now, but there have been in the past. He doesn't care whether his subjects are male, female, or animal. He only cares about the results."

Ruby nodded. "So you've never wished for someone quiet

and gentle who'll mend your socks for you and cook a good meal?"

"My father wanted that for me. I have to say that there are days when I think he was right. But then I see someone like you. Someone I thought couldn't exist, and I have to wonder."

Ruby couldn't help but notice that the moonlight caressed his hair as though he was someone special.

They reached the healer's cottage. The hunters who had been standing outside the cottage had gone, and there was only the lonely sound of wolfkin howling.

"We have a long night ahead of us," said the Huntsman. "We can take shifts watching the wolfkin."

"We?" asked Ruby. "I can handle this on my own."

"I'm sure you can. But since I'm staying the night here regardless, I might as well be of some use." He opened the door and went inside.

Ruby's heart sank. Her plans were now in ruins. How was she going to sneak out of the cottage with him there all night?

CHAPTER 42

The stench of burning flesh and fur were heavy in the air. The healer was sweating while he worked, even though it was the two hunters beside him who were doing the heavy work of moving the limp wolfkin into a cage.

Ruby opened the windows, not worried about bats or other creatures that might fly through. They had bigger concerns this night.

"Tyler, it's about time you came back," said the healer. "The king doesn't expect me to save this creature, does he? You told him it was mostly dead, right?"

Tyler. So he had a name other than the Huntsman.

It suited him, although it felt strangely intimate to think of him as Tyler instead of the Huntsman. Ruby wondered who was allowed to call him by that name.

"Relax, Magnus," said Tyler. "The king will do what he will do. No amount of talking can change that, so don't worry about it."

"Easy for you to say. Killing is easier than saving lives."

"Ah, it's like that, is it?" Tyler scratched his jaw. "It's been hours since you had a drink, hasn't it? You're getting grouchy."

"I had to use my last bottle to keep the wounds clean," said Magnus. "Couldn't you have shot him just once instead of three times? It would have made my job much easier."

"How is he?" asked Tyler.

"He's alive. Whether he'll stay that way is another question."

Magnus motioned for the men to lift the wolfkin cage onto his table. Lanson lay in his cage like the dead, but his furry rib cage rose and fell steadily with his breathing. Ruby was glad to see that he was no longer tied and muzzled.

"How long will it take for him to go back to normal?" asked Ruby.

"Assuming he lives?" asked Magnus. "Might never be normal. But he was never a normal creature to begin with, so your guess is as good as mine." He eyed her closely. "Better, maybe, if what the men tell me about you is true."

"It's not," said Tyler. He glared at his hunters. "Don't go spreading rumors. There's enough fear of the woods as it is without adding far-fetched stories to it."

The two hunters exchanged uneasy glances, then they nodded.

"Pass on the warning to the others," said Tyler.

The men nodded again.

"Go on, get some sleep," said Tyler. "Your wives must be getting worried by now."

The men mumbled their thanks and left.

"That's all I need to walk away from this?" asked Magnus. "A wife? Hell, I'll have to get myself one first thing in the morning. Oh, wait, I forgot. No woman would ever be crazy enough to live with me in a house full of monsters that get dragged in by the hunters in the middle of the night. Oh, and then there's the howling. Let's not forget that. Do you think I could find myself a deaf woman who could sleep like the dead when her home is full of screaming animals and bloody hunters?"

"Get some sleep, Magnus. You'll want to be fresh in the morning. You never know if the king might decide to visit his latest pets."

"The king?" Magnus groaned. "How am I supposed to sleep knowing that he might just show up anytime?"

Ruby went cold with the thought of seeing the king. He might take the wolfkin to someplace she couldn't reach. She needed to get everyone out tonight if she could.

"We'll wake you if we need you," said Tyler.

"You're staying here all night?" asked Magnus.

Tyler nodded.

"And her?"

"Her too. She may be able to make a poultice for the wounds if you tell her what to do."

Magnus threw a glare at Tyler. "No amount of poultice is going to heal an arrow wound deep into his vitals."

Ruby's heart sank. "Will he live?"

"We'll see." Magnus walked into the other room, looking like he was already asleep on his feet.

She'd been worried about how to get Lanson out when the others escaped. Now, she wondered if they'd have to leave him.

It was possible that they could wait a night or two to let Lanson recover, but she didn't know if she'd get another chance to open the cages. If they had to stay for days, who knew where they might all end up?

Magnus shut the door firmly. It was clear that he didn't want to be woken whether they needed him or not.

"Is he a good healer?" she asked doubtfully.

"He's the best. Far better than he pretends to be."

"Even on animals he wants dead?"

"He doesn't like to show it, but Magnus has a soft heart, especially for animals. I swear he likes creatures better than people."

"Even wolfkin?"

"I've never met a creature that Magnus didn't want to heal. It's in his blood. His father was a healer of animals, and so was his grandfather. He grew up among animals."

"Like you."

"True. My family killed them. His family saved them. It all depended on whether the king wanted a trophy or a new pet, I suppose." Tyler sat down on a chair by the fireplace. "We didn't know that when we were boys stealing pies together from the kitchen, though."

"Isn't stealing the king's pies a crime punishable by death?"

"I didn't say we were smart. Just lucky enough to survive this long." He gestured to the bench by the window. "I'll take first watch. There's a blanket beneath the bench. I've spent plenty of nights here to know that's not a comfortable bench, but it's better than the floor."

Ruby pulled out the thick woolen blanket from beneath the bench. It smelled of alcohol but seemed reasonably clean otherwise. All she cared about was that it was warm and thick and big enough to wrap around her.

She hadn't realized how chilled she was until she curled up in the blanket. She noticed Tyler watching her.

"My mother made that blanket for Magnus's mother."

"It's wonderful." Ruby pulled the blanket tighter. "She must have been quite talented."

"I don't remember her, but I like to think she was."

The wolfkin huffed. Ruby wondered if he was conscious and listening.

She closed her eyes, pretending to sleep. She listened to Lanson's labored breathing. His cage had the same latch as the others, but unless he could run, Ruby wouldn't be able to escape with him.

What was she supposed to do now?

CHAPTER 43

Tyler watched Ruby pretend to sleep on her bench. Her chest rose and fell steadily, but he could sense her alertness in the same way he could sense it when an animal was aware of his presence.

She was hiding something. It could be the obvious thing —some plan for escape brewing in her mind—but he thought there might be more to it.

He'd seen plenty of captives of all kinds—animal, people, and everything in between. Most of them seemed to think that they were the only captive to ever cook up a plan for escape. There were some who simply gave up, but they were the exceptions, and their hopelessness showed plainly in their eyes.

Ruby had something else going on. Despite her cooperation, she was worried about how she might escape. That had bothered him from the beginning. She hadn't run when they found her in the woods, which made sense at the time. Who wouldn't prefer human company to wolfkin? The hunters would at least be able to get her out of the forest.

But since then, she had shown that she wasn't afraid of

the wolfkin. She seemed to be worried about them in a way he'd never seen—the injured one in particular.

He should be interrogating her. But he was so tired. Not just in body, but in spirit. What difference did it make if he dragged information out of her? He'd rather watch her curl up in his mother's blanket with her flame-colored hair spread across it.

These were treasonous thoughts. No woman could come before the king, not if you were the king's huntsman or healer or cook. The Dark King demanded all from his subjects.

For one night, Tyler had hoped to carve out a few moments for himself. For his father. For what might have been with a girl if only life had been different.

But the night would not last forever. When the dawn came, he would have to take on his duties as the king's huntsman, and Ruby would go back to being a prisoner. He had no choice but to accept the inevitable as he had done so many times.

So why did he feel a thin thread of hope?

He must be a fool. Or it was late and he was exhausted. Or the woman was having an effect on him that he couldn't afford.

This was the second time in one night that he'd felt it. Hope for what, he couldn't fathom. His father was beyond his reach. Even Ruby's beautiful humming couldn't soothe him.

Now that he thought of it, though, it did affect Father. Not in the way Tyler had hoped. It seemed to make Father more agitated than ever. But that was an effect, wasn't it?

Had some part of his father recognized the old lullaby?

Tyler had stopped the experiment because Ruby clearly wasn't soothing his father. But what if Father was agitated because it woke the human part of him? What if he was struggling against the beast in him?

Hope was a dangerous thing in the Kingdom of Midnight, especially when it came to Tyler's father. Even if Ruby managed to affect Father, it wouldn't be all good news. The king would take a keen interest in anything she did, if he learned that she could manage the howlers.

He watched Ruby breathe while she slept. Her breathing had changed enough for Tyler to know she was truly asleep now. There was something dangerously innocent about that.

She was in enemy territory with her captor in the room. Yet she trusted enough to sleep, simply because he had told her that he would take the first watch.

A lock of Ruby's hair had fallen over her eyes. It was silky and reflected the fire's glow, but it kept him from seeing whether her eyes were completely closed. He could tell by her breathing that she was asleep now, but every hunter knew that it was better to use all his senses.

Tyler got up and approached Ruby. He gently reached over to move her hair out of her face. He didn't want to wake her. Despite being her captor and having a good reason to move her hair out of her eyes, he would feel awkward if she woke to find him so close.

A low growl vibrated the air from behind.

Tyler froze with his hand midway to Ruby's face.

The injured wolfkin snarled at him from inside the cage. He was still lying on his side but managed to make it clear that he was still a monster that could mangle a man in a single swipe.

Tyler had his knives on him but not his bow. He'd need more than a single blade to take down a wolfkin. He had to remind himself that this one was caged and weak.

Tyler moved his hand away and took a step back.

The wolfkin stopped growling but watched him, looking like he'd love nothing better than to have Tyler for dinner.

Tyler took a step toward Ruby and experimentally reached out his hand to her face again.

The wolfkin snarled, more fiercely this time. This wasn't just a warning—there was anger behind his growl.

Shadow whined outside the door where Tyler had left him. Dogs did not do well in the presence of wolfkin, so Tyler had tied Shadow to a post outside. He must have sensed that something was happening.

Just to be sure, Tyler moved his hand closer to Ruby.

The wolfkin pushed himself up and snapped and growled, showing fangs that were the size of kitchen knives.

The table beneath him rocked, threatening to topple over. It was a sturdy table, meant to hold panicked animals. But like most of Magnus's equipment, it was a holdover from the old days when Magnus's father treated farm animals. It was never meant to hold a monster like a wolfkin.

Ruby woke up and rushed toward the cage as soon as she saw what was happening.

Tyler grabbed her arm to hold her back. The cage rattled as the wolfkin slammed into it. The cottage filled with growls and the rattling of the cage.

Outside, Shadow barked frantically while the captured wolfkin howled. The howlers also joined in with their tortured, almost-human voices.

"What in blasted wild fairy forest is going on?" Magnus stumbled out of the other room, fumbling with his trousers.

"Shh," said Ruby to the wolfkin. She ignored Tyler, who was still holding her arm to keep her from getting too close.

Ruby gave Tyler a pointed look. They both knew that she could get out of his hold if she wished, but she was giving him the chance to do it voluntarily.

"Don't get too close," he said as he let her go.

She didn't touch the cage, but she got closer than Tyler liked.

Ruby put her hands out toward the cage. "It's all right. You're all right. They're patching up your wounds. Lie down and rest. Shh."

She kept her voice gentle and soothing. There wasn't an ounce of fear in her.

The wolfkin continued to growl, but it was clear he was growling at Tyler and not at Ruby.

"It's all right. You need your rest. I'm right here. I'll be right next to you all night. These men are here to heal you."

The wolfkin's growl lowered to a rumble as though he understood her words.

It bothered Tyler that the monster seemed to understand Ruby better than Father understood Tyler. Had the king's dark sorcerers done such a poor job with their magic that they'd botched every aspect of the transformation?

"Lie down." Ruby's voice was becoming more authoritative. "You're not going to get better like this, and there's nothing you can do in that cage anyway, so just rest."

With one last growl directed at Tyler, the wolfkin lay back down in his cage.

Outside, the wolfkin soon stopped howling. Shadow kept barking, though, and the twisted howlers continued to sing out. Tyler wondered if his father was one of them.

Magnus stared at Ruby with wide eyes. "I could use an assistant like you."

"She's taken," said Tyler, sounding more annoyed than he'd intended.

"You don't need another assistant," said Magnus. "She clearly has talent with beasts. Can you say the same for her talents as a hunter?"

"I can, as a matter of fact. The woman has many talents."

Magnus quirked a brow at Tyler but didn't argue. It both

annoyed Tyler and made him a little proud that Ruby's talents were so special. It also worried him that there would be no way to keep the king from noticing it as well.

Ruby was whispering to the wolfkin. Soothing words to try to keep him calm and relaxed.

There was no doubt in Tyler's mind now that Ruby didn't just have a way with the monsters—the wolfkin considered her part of their pack.

CHAPTER 44

*T*he whole plan was blown. Ruby had hoped to keep everything seeming normal until it was time to free the wolfkin. Instead, she'd brought too much attention to herself. Tyler and Magnus were staring at her with an intensity that let her know that she wouldn't be able to sneak around unnoticed.

She tried to concentrate on the bright side. Lanson seemed well enough to get up and make a nuisance of himself, which was remarkable after being shot three times. And she'd managed to get him to settle down again.

Ruby avoided looking at Tyler. This entire night was not going the way she had hoped. It was beginning to look like she might have to accept that they were all stuck here for a few days until she could find a way to release the wolfkin.

"I'll take my shift," she said. "I might as well let you sleep, since I'm wide awake now."

Tyler looked like he was on the verge of turning down her offer, but then agreed. He must be exhausted. He didn't strike her as the kind of man to let someone else be on watch on a night like this.

She took Tyler's chair while he lay on the bench beneath the window. Lying on his side, facing her, he pulled the blanket over him. She assumed he'd want to keep an eye on her, but he needn't have bothered. She couldn't see a way to get out with Lanson still in his condition anyway.

Just before Tyler closed his eyes, he took a deep breath through his nose as though taking in the scent of the blanket.

She understood. She'd do the same if she'd had a blanket that her mother had made. It must be hard for him to leave it here in this messy place where animals could soil it.

He lay with his eyes closed, breathing steadily. She couldn't tell if he slept or not. She guessed he wasn't the type to snore. He was a man who was an expert at being quiet and still.

She understood why the Dark King had chosen Tyler to be his monster hunter. Except that the monster in the cage wasn't the monster Tyler thought he was.

The wolfkin was watching her. Lanson had been almost dead when they brought him in. If he'd been an ordinary man, the arrow wounds would have killed him. If he'd been an ordinary wolf, it would have killed him too.

Lanson looked considerably better than when they'd brought him in. His wolf eyes were clear, and he lay on his belly rather than on his side. Ruby couldn't imagine how much that hurt.

The wolfkin pawed silently toward the cage door.

He was sending her a message. He could take the pain. He could run.

Maybe he could. Or maybe he couldn't. Just because a creature was stubborn didn't mean that his body could handle what he demanded of it.

She'd have only one shot. Tyler was a hunter who'd trained all his life. If she made one small sound, she was sure he'd wake up. He was so close that even a squeak of the floorboards might wake him.

Ruby shook her head at the wolfkin and gestured toward Tyler.

The wolfkin pulled back his lips and showed his fangs in a silent snarl. He snapped his jaws at Tyler.

He wanted her to kill Tyler.

She almost laughed at that. Tyler was a master huntsman. There was no chance that she could sneak up on him to slit his throat, even if she wanted to, which she definitely did not.

Ruby shook her head again. In addition to the worry that she would wake Tyler up if she tried to let out Lanson, she now worried that Lanson might attack Tyler.

She wondered what to do. In the end, she decided that the best thing she could do was to find the other wolfkin cages. That would ensure that she knew where they were for when the time came.

She wanted to tell the other wolfkin that Lanson was alive and recovering. Most importantly, she wanted to visit her grandmother to make sure she was all right.

Ruby listened to Tyler's steady breathing for a long time. She waited until she was sure that Tyler was fully asleep. Then she did her best to be silent as she got up and snuck over to the door. She glanced one last time at Tyler.

He lay beneath the window, looking serene and relaxed. It was an intimate feeling to watch a man sleep. He held on to his mother's blanket, making sure it didn't slip away.

Ruby quietly opened the door and left the cottage.

CHAPTER 45

Tyler wasn't surprised that Ruby snuck out as soon as she thought he was asleep, but he was disappointed.

The disappointment had nothing to do with her wanting to sneak away. He might even have lost respect for her if she hadn't tried to escape.

What bothered him was that she snuck away while spending the night with him. Had he such little effect on her that she wanted to leave as soon as she thought he was asleep? Had she no respect for his skills as a hunter?

He sighed as soon as she left the cottage. He hadn't been fully asleep, but he had been drifting. The cottage was warm and there were few moments in life when he could curl up beneath his mother's blanket and have a girl like Ruby in the room watching him sleep. It was oddly comforting.

Sure, he knew that she was a prisoner with the skills to slit his throat if that was what she wanted. He'd even been foolish enough to leave her armed.

He didn't think she'd hurt anyone, though. She'd never attacked any of her trainers, even during the days when she thought they'd meant to feed her to the wolfkin. He could be wrong, though. She certainly had the skills to kill if she wished.

He reluctantly pushed back his mother's blanket. As he got up from his bench, the wolfkin snarled at him. The creature seemed much stronger than before.

Wolfkin must heal faster than ordinary creatures. That would be a piece of information that the king would be particularly interested in. The Dark King could lead an army of monsters that could recover in mere hours from what would normally be a killing blow. That was enough to put fear into his enemies as well as his allies.

An army like that could be unstoppable by anything other than an army of wild fairies. And even then, it would be an even bet as to who might win.

As Tyler left the cottage to follow Ruby, the blasted howlers began howling. So much for stealth.

The other creatures picked up the noise. Even his own hunting dogs began to bark and howl.

He really needed to move the kennel out farther from the other creatures. Not only could they hear each other, he was sure they could smell each other. That probably kept all the beasts in a constant state of agitation.

He'd never intended to be a menagerie keeper. But then again, he never should have been a monster hunter, either.

He silently stalked Ruby the way he would a deer in the forest. She was good. Good enough that he wondered if he should recruit her as one of his hunters.

She moved from shadow to shadow. Of course, with all the howling, she could be singing and he wouldn't hear her. But he could tell by her stealthy movements that she'd at least had some training in the art of being in enemy territory.

She might not be good enough to fool an animal in the forest, but she had the basic skills. Her grandmother had done a good job training her. He wanted to meet her someday.

Tyler expected Ruby to either walk to the courtyard or to the forest. She knew both paths. They were dangerous, but either way would take her out of the castle, if she could survive the journey.

But she didn't head in either of those directions. Instead, she walked further into the wolfkin yard.

The hunters had begun calling it the wolfkin yard in an unusual fit of optimism. The name stuck, even after it became full of howlers selected from the king's dungeons. To actually have it contain wild beasts from the dark forest was a wonder.

It was perhaps the most dangerous place in the castle, aside from the king's own chambers and the dungeon. Ruby had no business being here, and Tyler was tempted to stop this foolishness and haul her back.

But his curiosity was undeniable. So he followed her as she moved deeper into the row of cages.

At the far end of the yard were the wild wolfkin cages. His men had placed the new captives near the old ones. He saw that they'd left the two new ones crammed in the single cage they'd come in. He didn't blame them. It would be quite the dangerous production to get one of them out.

Ruby did a strange thing. She walked straight to the cage with the silver wolfkin and knelt in front of it. She whispered something into the cage.

Tyler would have given anything to hear what she said. The foolish girl then leaned her head too close to the cage. Tyler almost called out. It would be too late, though, if the wolfkin wanted to harm her.

The monstrous, wolflike beast licked Ruby's forehead.

Tyler squinted. Had he just seen what he thought he saw?

Ruby put her hand into the cage.

Tyler was too far away to stop her. He was about to witness her being torn apart.

Instead, the wolfkin allowed her to caress its neck.

Tyler had to remember to breathe. He blinked several times, but the image of Ruby sitting in the moonlight petting a wolfkin didn't change. It was truly happening.

Who was she?

Thoughts of wild fairies and dangerous creatures from the forest filled his mind. But he couldn't think of any stories that described a beautiful girl who befriended monsters.

Ruby reluctantly stood up, and Tyler could swear she was saying goodbye to the beast. Then she walked over to the cage with the newly captured wolfkin.

He was afraid that she'd stick her hand between the bars or lean her head against the cage again, but she didn't. She whispered to these wolfkin too, but she held herself back and kept a small distance from them.

She obviously felt closer to the wolfkin in the first cage. That was odd. When Tyler brought her here before their hunt, she'd barely glanced at the silver wolfkin.

The wolfkin made noises that sounded like the grumblings certain breeds of dogs made. Those dog owners swore their dogs talked, although they had no idea what the dogs were saying. Did Ruby understand them?

As if to answer his question, Ruby turned and searched the shadows until she saw him. Her beasts must have smelled him.

Tyler stepped out of the shadows and into the moonlight. It was time to get some answers.

CHAPTER 46

*R*uby's heart skipped far too many beats when she saw Tyler stepping out of the shadows.

The wolfkin growled when they saw him, but they'd known about him long before she did. She'd been caught.

Ruby had a crazy impulse to let the wolfkin out and run. But if she did that, she would guarantee a bloody battle. She didn't know how many would escape, but she knew it wouldn't be enough. Of course, at this rate, no one was going to escape.

"Whatever it is you're planning, I don't think it's a good idea, not if you want to live." Tyler kept his voice low.

"I wasn't planning anything. I just wanted to visit the wolfkin and make sure they were all right."

"Enough lies. Tell me what is happening here. How are you able to talk to the wolfkin? Are you a witch?"

"Me?" Ruby pointed to herself. "Not at all."

The thought was so silly that she would have laughed if it wasn't so dangerous. Tyler could have her killed with a word.

"Then how are you controlling the monsters? What are you planning?"

Ruby searched her thoughts for anything that might help her out of this situation. But the only thing that came to mind was the truth.

"Do you know that the howlers used to be people?" she asked.

Tyler stilled. He knew. "Who told you that?"

She walked toward him. She didn't want to have to shout to be heard. "That howler you showed me earlier—the one you wanted me to hum to—was that someone you knew? Someone you once cared about?" She was casting about for anything that might make him understand.

"What does it matter?"

"What if they had a place to go? What if they could be reunited with their families?"

He scoffed. "What are you talking about? They are the king's property. What you speak of is treason."

"What if I committed treason, and you turned a blind eye to it?"

"Then I would be a traitor surely as you. Why would I even consider such a thing?"

"Because that howler you care about is going to spend the rest of his life living in that cage like a crazed animal."

His face turned to stone. It was a harsh thing to say, but sometimes, harsh truths needed to be said.

"I suppose you're going to try to convince me that you have something better for him," said Tyler.

"Perhaps. I can't make promises, but I can tell you that he'll be treated with more respect, more...like a person than the way he is now."

She wasn't sure that being chained to a column and being fed by children was better than what Tyler had done for his howler. But she sensed that there was hope for the howlers at the wolfkin mansion that didn't exist here.

Tyler watched her for a moment before asking, "Can they fix him?"

Ruby hesitated. "I don't know."

"Then that's no better than being here. At least here, I can make sure he's cared for."

"But what about the others? Who will care for them?"

"I can't fix the kingdom's problems. I can only try to deal with my own. And you are now one of mine. If you don't get back to the cottage and forget all this, you'll end up being executed for treason."

He was doing her a favor by not having her executed right here and now.

"And if I do go quietly back to the cottage?"

"Then I'll consider forgetting about this incident."

Ruby nodded.

The two of them walked back toward the healer's cottage. Everywhere they went, there were growls and howls. When they walked through the dog kennels, there was a lot of barking as well.

"The whole castle must be awake by now," said Tyler. He picked up his speed.

Then they both suddenly stopped at the sight ahead of them.

A group of guards dressed in crimson finery were heading to the healer's cottage. The guards carried torches that bathed their leader in red light.

The Dark King was on his way to the cottage.

He was as intimidating as Ruby had always heard. His guards looked deadly and somehow inhuman despite their human form. It must be their armor and the moonlight, but the overall effect was that they looked like bloodthirsty guards from the underworld.

Ruby had to catch her breath to comprehend what was

happening. The small cottage looked insignificant and flimsy compared to the authority of the guards. She couldn't tell if it was a raid, or if the king was bestowing an honor on the healer.

Tyler walked bravely forward and bent his knee to the king. "Your Majesty."

"This is where my beasts are?" asked the king.

In the torchlight, his infamous cloak of skins seemed to shift and move, as though the souls of the patches were still being cut by the king's sword. Ruby could almost feel the anguish of the king's enemies sewn into that cloak.

"The injured one is here, Your Majesty," said Tyler. "The others are in cages in the yard. There will be more light for you to see them in the morning."

"I'm here now. Clearly the beasts want me here, since they're howling so loudly."

Tyler bowed his head and opened the door for the king. The cottage was small and didn't have room for so many people.

The king entered, and Tyler followed.

Ruby wasn't sure what she was supposed to do. The guards watched her. Their faces were covered with their helms, so she couldn't tell if they were truly human. All she could see were their eyes reflecting the torchlight and mouths that were as hard and controlled as their bodies.

Ruby's heart hammered. The howling and barking didn't help. It just added to the cacophony of her thoughts and the rising panic.

Would they stop her if she slipped back into the darkness? Even though this was the worst time to escape, she couldn't help but want to. She slowly shifted back, taking a step closer to the shadow.

The king's guards instantly turned and glared at her. Ruby stopped and tried to look innocent.

The king came out of the cottage, followed by Tyler and Magnus.

"...training to start in the morning," the king was saying. "I want them eating out of my hands and obeying my slightest wish."

"Yes, Your Majesty." The men spoke and bowed together. Ruby noticed that Tyler's bow was stiff and reluctant.

"One more thing," said the king. "I want the howlers to be readied for travel tomorrow."

"Travel to where, Your Majesty?" asked Tyler.

"It's time they earned their keep. I'm sending them to Everness." The king chuckled. "Let's see how their golden lances and scented handkerchiefs handle a shipment of howlers loose in their fields."

"How many should I prepare, Your Majesty?" asked Tyler.

"All of them."

"All?" Tyler stiffened. "But, Your Majesty—"

"Yes, yes, of course. I have not forgotten your father. You may spare him and continue to pamper him in your little garden. That is your reward for finally capturing my wolfkin. It's a good start, but let us not forget that the goal is to have an army."

His father.

It made sense now why Tyler took such good care of that particular howler. Ruby's heart went out to him. It must have been impossibly hard to watch his father become a tortured creature made with dark magic.

Tyler bowed stiffly as the Dark King left with his entourage of fire and steel.

CHAPTER 47

*H*is father had been spared.

The thought rattled around Tyler's head, but he could gain little comfort from it. He'd only been spared because Tyler had captured the wolfkin. That had been nothing but luck and completely out of Tyler's control.

If he wanted to keep his father alive, he'd need to capture more wolfkin. How was he going to manage that?

Capturing enough for a wolfkin army was impossible. But the Dark King lived and breathed impossibilities every day. Wasn't that why he had his sorcerers? Wasn't that how he'd managed to win the Wild Wars against the fairies?

Tyler wasn't even sure who the king wanted to use his wolfkin army against. No one threatened the Kingdom of Midnight. No one wanted it, as far as Tyler could tell. It was surrounded by the forest, which none but the bravest souls dared to cross, and that was only with the king's permission.

If the king was releasing the howlers in Everness, that did not necessarily mean that he wanted to conquer their neighboring kingdom. He might just be entertained by the thought of causing so much trouble in the fabled golden kingdom of sunshine and laughter.

Still, the end result was that Tyler's father would be the only howler left. When the king's dark sorcerers needed something for the king's ongoing experiments—a nail clipping, blood, or even an entire howler to sacrifice—there would be no one else left other than Tyler's father.

A cold wind blew from the direction of the forest as if to remind him that it was there. A huntsman's life was inevitably intertwined with the forest. He thought that there was a time when the forest wasn't so hostile, a time before the Dark King's reign, before the Wild Wars. But those easy times were gone, and only hard choices remained.

Ruby walked past him to go into the cottage. He guessed that she was going in to check on the injured beast.

Her concern for the wolfkin was interesting. He'd known people like that. The kitchen maids sometimes got attached to Shadow, to the point where Tyler had to step in to make sure his dog didn't get too fat.

He stood outside for a moment longer, watching the king's entourage march into the night.

What would it mean to free his father? Would he run wild through the forest like an animal? Or would he come back to haunt his old life as though he was still a man?

Whatever his life would be like, Tyler knew one thing— his father would be free. Even if it was only for one night, he would be outside of that cage. Would he live longer out there with his kind than here with Tyler?

Tyler had thought so. Now, he wasn't so sure.

"Holy mother of gerbils, my heart nearly stopped when the king walked into my cottage," said Magnus. He'd been quietly watching the king's procession disappear into the darkness as well.

"Actually, it's *his* cottage," said Tyler.

"He owns my toes and fingers too, but that won't keep me from calling them mine. You said he *might* come in the morning. You didn't say anything about the middle of the blasted night."

"I know this will come as a shock to you, Magnus, but the king does not consult me on his schedule."

"I didn't even have time to put my shoes on."

"I saw that."

"I need a drink." Magnus pushed open his door with a trembling hand.

Tyler didn't remind him that he'd used his last bottle on the wolfkin's wounds.

Inside, Ruby was softly speaking to the wolfkin. It was a soothing sound, but it didn't seem to calm the creature. The wolfkin was on his feet, trying to break out of the cage. He was so big that he could barely stand in the cage, but that didn't stop him from slamming against the sides.

"How could he have recovered so fast?" asked Tyler.

"It wasn't anything I did," said Magnus, making a protective gesture in the old ways.

Magnus had never even been religious or superstitious, as far as Tyler knew. Seeing the wolfkin had a way of converting people to anything that might protect their soul, though. He'd seen it plenty of times with his hunters.

"What did the king do to him?" asked Ruby. "Did he use his dark magic on him?"

Tyler shook his head. "Not that I saw. The wolfkin leapt up as soon as the king came in. He doesn't seem to like the king."

The wolfkin shook the entire table with his slamming. There wasn't room for him to pull back much before a slam, so it was more of a harassing of the cage than anything else.

"That's my da's table," said Magnus. "I knew I should have made you put him outside."

"We'll watch him and take care of any problems," said Tyler. "Go back to bed and get some sleep. Tomorrow will be a big day."

Magnus grumbled, but Tyler knew that he didn't want to be near an angry wolfkin any more than he had to. Tyler waited until Magnus went into the other room and shut the door before turning to Ruby.

He motioned for her to follow him outside. When Tyler was sure that Magnus couldn't hear their conversation, he whispered so softly that she had to lean in to hear him.

"Where would you plan to take the howlers if you could free them?" asked Tyler.

Ruby looked deep into his eyes. Tyler didn't try to hide anything. If this remarkable girl wanted to search for truth in his eyes, he was fine with letting her see whatever she might find.

She was beautiful in the moonlight. He couldn't think of a more dangerous time for him to be besotted by her beauty, but he couldn't help but notice it.

Her hair shone like a fire in the night. Her eyes were full of surprise and cautious hope. He could spend the rest of his life getting lost in those eyes.

His father had once told him about what it was like when he met Tyler's mother. He described it in a way that was so out of character for his father. He spoke of the summer flowers, the sunshine that lasted until bedtime, and his mother's blue eyes that were bluer than the sky, deeper than the sea. Father had talked about how he'd lost himself in those eyes.

That had been the night of her funeral. Tyler had never heard his father speak like that before. He knew even then that his father would never talk like that again. But Tyler remembered the pain, love, loss, and memories of joy—all mixed together in Father's voice.

Tyler had assumed that when he grew up, he would find

someone that he felt that deeply for. But he hadn't found anyone close to that.

When the king punished Father for not being able to capture a wolfkin, Tyler had put aside all those childish thoughts. There was no room for anything other than duty. Shadow was the most extravagant emotional indulgence he'd allowed himself.

He watched Ruby's lips part as she began to answer him. They were full and red, and they filled his world. He had a hard time even remembering what his question was.

Before she could answer him, he leaned over and kissed her.

*a*t first, Tyler wasn't sure how Ruby would receive him. He could feel her stiffen in surprise as he pressed his lips against hers.

Then her lips opened and her hands drifted up to touch his chest. Even through the leather, he could feel her warmth, as if she touched his heart directly.

His whole world filled with the touch of her lips, and he breathed in her feminine scent.

It was a stolen moment for himself in a lifetime of duty to others. He let it linger, living in the moment like never before.

Then he reluctantly pulled back. He'd just complicated his life and hers far beyond what was wise.

She leaned toward him with her eyes closed, which he liked far too much. Then he saw her coming out of her plea-sure-filled daze and come back to herself again. He felt a pang of disappointment.

Her cheeks flamed enough for him to see it even in the moonlight. She opened her mouth to say something, then closed it.

Had he been her first kiss? He couldn't imagine it, but there was a part of him that liked the idea that no other man had tasted her. Tyler put his hand out to her hot cheek and caressed it with his thumb.

"What am I going to do with you?" he asked.

He thought for sure that she would say, "Set me free."

Instead, she said, "Come with me."

"Go with you where?" he asked, genuinely puzzled.

"Anywhere is better than here. Let me free the captives, then come with us."

She looked at him in all earnestness. She had no idea what she was asking him to do.

There was the king, certainly. Betraying the king and stealing his beasts were no light offenses. The king wouldn't simply have the betrayer killed—he'd make sure to torture him slowly first to make a splendid example of him.

Even if Tyler could escape the king's wrath, what would he do? His family had been the royal huntsman for generations. He had never thought about living another kind of life.

A candle flickered on in Magnus's window. Both Tyler and Ruby became silent, watching the healer's shadow as he got up out of bed.

Magnus bent, seemingly rummaging through something. Then he put a small flask near his lips and tipped his head back, sticking his tongue out to catch the last drips from the flask.

Tyler sighed. Magnus's family had been animal healers for as many generations as Tyler's. They'd grown up together, both proud of their heritage and equally trapped by it.

Magnus had found his own escape through the bottle, but that was no less of a deadly trap.

Tyler had thought that Ruby didn't understand his situation, but as he watched the dim shadow of his old friend

Magnus, he thought that maybe she understood more than he'd thought.

"That howler in the garden—that's your father, isn't he?"

Tyler became very still. He barely dared to breathe. No one ever talked to him about his father's situation, other than the Dark King.

"I heard what the king said to you," she said. "Don't you want to free him?"

"And where would he go?" That came out with more anger than he'd intended, but he was tired of trying to come up with solutions. "That would doom him forever. Dark magic got him that way, and only the king's sorcerers can turn him back."

"You think they'll turn him back for you one day?"

Tyler couldn't answer that, not out loud. Of course they wouldn't turn his father back. He wasn't sure that they could, even if they wanted to. The king's sorcerers did their best to turn people into wolfkin, not the other way around.

Despite their efforts, all they had was a yard full of howlers. Tyler shuddered to think about what the result might be if they ever tried to reverse it.

There were stories of the king and his sorcerers bringing back dead soldiers to try to build an army of the dead. Those stories made Tyler glad to be the royal huntsman rather than the poor soul in charge of the resurrected.

He knew one thing for sure. Whatever the king's dark magic touched, it turned into an abomination.

"Come with me," whispered Ruby in her maddeningly tempting voice. "There's a place...I'm sure they would take you and your father, if you set the captives free. It's a place with others like him and their families."

Tyler couldn't look at her and think clearly at the same time. Was he even considering such treason and thievery? Poaching the king's game was punishable by death. He couldn't even imagine what the punishment would be for taking all his wolfkin and howlers. Tyler would be a fugitive for life.

Through the window, Magnus's shadow hunched and began to rock back and forth. Tyler frowned, not understanding what Magnus was doing.

Then he heard his old friend's broken sobs.

Tyler let out a long breath and stared at the ground, listening to his friend sobbing. It was a hushed, secret sound, full of emotions Magnus could never say.

On the far side of the yard, a lone howler screeched at the moon, the sound full of frustration and anguish. Tyler wondered if that was his father.

CHAPTER 49

*R*uby didn't know that she could feel so many emotions at the same time.

He'd said yes.

And he'd kissed her. Saints above, he'd kissed her.

Her mind still reeled. She could still hear his voice, telling her that he'd go with her. That he'd help her free the captives.

She could still feel the warmth of his lips, making her own tingle with the memory.

Her grandmother's voice cautioned her in her head. This could be a trap. He might even go as far as freeing the captives, only to betray them once he discovered where the wolfkin mansion was.

But Gran had also told Ruby that you had to trust your instincts. Because in both life and in battle, it was far better to go through it with people who would watch your back. The first step to that was figuring out who to trust.

No matter what her brain said, she instinctively trusted Tyler. Besides, she couldn't think of a way to escape the castle without his cooperation. She couldn't even get away long enough to open any of the cages on her own.

Tyler had his conditions, though. He insisted on taking Magnus with them, even though he wasn't a captive here. Ruby didn't think the wolfkin would mind having a healer on their side.

They stood in front of Lanson's cage and quickly explained that Tyler and Magnus were going to help them. Tyler refused to open the cage until the wolfkin agreed to his conditions.

Ruby held her breath while Tyler laid out his terms. Safety and shelter for his father, Magnus, Tyler and Ruby for as long as they wished. It touched her that he included her as part of his bargain. He made Lanson agree to the terms by nodding to each name.

Then came the moment of truth. Ruby could have opened the cage herself, but she felt that Tyler should do it. If he truly did not want to do this, he would likely find himself unable to open that cage.

But Tyler was both a man of his word and a man of action. He opened the cage without hesitation.

Ruby swelled a little with admiration as she watched him. He was perhaps the bravest person she'd ever met, aside from her grandmother.

She placed her hand on her knife hilt, just in case. She wasn't sure which one she'd be willing to harm if there was a fight, but she knew she couldn't allow either one to kill the other.

When the cage opened, Lanson did not attack. And neither did Tyler. Ruby let out a breath she didn't know she'd been holding.

Lanson moved stiffly and allowed Ruby and Tyler to help him down from the table where the cage was situated. The fact that he could move at all was astonishing. He was near death only a few hours ago.

"The king would have been very pleased to know how

quickly a wolfkin heals," said Tyler wistfully.

"What are you doing?" Magnus stood in the doorway, looking shocked and scared.

"It's all right, Magnus." Tyler never took his eyes off Lanson as the wolfkin stretched his muscles. He never took his hand off his knife, either.

"Are you crazy?" asked Magnus. "You just freed the most dangerous beast in the yard." He slowly backed away behind his door.

The wolfkin walked out through the open front door into the night. Both Ruby and Tyler breathed a sigh of relief and finally took their hands off their knives.

"Listen, Magnus, we're switching sides."

The healer stared at Tyler, looking dumbfounded.

"You want to die miserable and broken like your father?" asked Tyler. "I don't want to turn into a howler, or worse, like *my* father. Our heritage is gone, Magnus. There's nothing for us here but rot and ruin. Come with me. Let's start a new life together."

"A life that lasts half a night?" asked Magnus.

Ruby could tell this was going to be a longer conversation than she had time for. Now that Lanson was out and moving, she felt the urgency.

"I'll be out opening cages," she said. "Come find me when you're finished here."

"What?" asked Magnus. That seemed to jolt him awake. "Is she insane? Those monsters will tear her to pieces. Are you really going to...?"

Ruby ran out the door and into the yard. The air was chill but fresh. Tyler had a challenging job ahead of him, trying to convince his friend to come along. Whether he managed it or not, Ruby hoped it would conclude sooner rather than later. She could use another pair of hands to open the cages.

She was tempted to begin opening cages as soon as she

neared them, but that would be dangerous without backup. She ran to the far end of the yard where the true wolfkin were. On the way there, she saw Lanson sitting on his haunches in the shadows.

"Can you run when it's time?" she asked.

He gave a low woof. She took that to mean yes, because she didn't have the luxury of thinking it was anything else.

Ruby ran to her grandmother's cage. She let her out first, knowing that there was still a chance that this silver wolf might not be her grandmother.

When the silver wolfkin was free, though, she licked Ruby's face. Ruby hugged her. Gran's thick fur was soft and plush.

Ruby wished she could spend more time with Gran, but she had to let the other wolfkin out. As she opened their cages, she told them about Lanson and the deal he had struck with Tyler.

One of the wolfkin lifted his leg and urinated rudely as she told him about the deal.

"I don't care what you think of it," said Ruby. "Lanson made the deal, and you'll stick by it if you know what's good for you."

The wolfkin—who Ruby guessed was Ketter—growled at her. Ruby's grandmother growled right back at him.

"You want me to open the cages or not?"

Ketter stopped growling.

"I'm not above walking away right now."

Ketter growled again, causing Gran to growl more ferociously. Ketter backed off.

"You need to stick with Lanson's deal. You have a problem with it, you talk to him."

Ketter sighed.

"Come on, I need your backup to let out the first howler."

Not giving Ketter the satisfaction of seeing her look back, Ruby ran toward the fenced garden to free Tyler's father.

CHAPTER 50

y the time Tyler finally convinced Magnus to join him, Ruby had gone. Tyler rushed out of the healer's cottage, dragging Magnus behind him.

It wasn't that Magnus didn't want to go. He just wanted to pack up all his gear. But there was no time for that. Tyler only allowed him to put on his shoes while Tyler collected whatever equipment he could grab and stuff into Magnus's bag.

On his way out, Tyler snatched up his mother's blanket and tied it over one shoulder and across his chest. Over that, he slung his bow and arrows.

Outside, the air was filled with howls. Some of the howlers were slamming against their cages, roaring as though they thought they were lions.

Ruby had said they were going to set them free, but Tyler was glad that she wasn't foolish enough to open the cages on her own. He had a feeling she'd free the captured wolfkin first, so he ran there. Along the way, he saw the injured wolfkin sitting silently in the shadows.

Magnus slowed when he saw the wolfkin. He watched the beast with a professional eye.

"Let's hope he remembers our deal," whispered Tyler as he slowed to a walk.

It wasn't wise to run in front of a predator. He didn't want to trigger its chasing instincts.

Magnus, who knew as well as Tyler just how dangerous an injured beast could be, slowly approached the wolfkin.

"What are you doing?" asked Tyler.

"Seeing if my patient is all right." Even with a cold breeze, sweat beaded on Magnus's brow and glistened in the moonlight. He was no fool. He understood the risk he was taking.

"Maybe he wants to be left alone, Magnus."

"Maybe he's bleeding and needs to be patched up. You said he understood and agreed to my safety."

"Yeah, but I didn't say he liked you. Come on, Magnus. Let him be."

With his muscles looking stiff with tension, Magnus gingerly continued to step closer to the wolfkin. The monstrous beast simply sat and watched, breathing shallowly.

Tyler got his bow ready and nocked an arrow. His motions were slow to not startle the monster. But if Ruby was right and the wolfkin was aware, he'd know exactly what Tyler was doing.

He aimed at the wolfkin's eye as Magnus kneeled beside the beast. Tyler held his breath to see if the monster would kill his old friend.

"I just want to make sure your wounds aren't bleeding," said Magnus, keeping his voice calm and soothing. "I'm here to help you, if you need it."

He put his hands out to the wolfkin. They were trembling in the moonlight. Tyler didn't know if that was from the lack of the drink Magnus so desperately needed or if it was all from fear. He hoped it was fear.

The wolfkin lay on his side, allowing Magnus to access his wounds.

Tyler let out a long breath and lowered his bow. Magnus took a moment to hunch over his knees, taking shuddering breaths. When he reached out to the wolfkin, his hands were steady.

Good ol' Magnus. There was no one as dedicated to saving beasts as he was. The old hunters used to say that there were none as well suited to their professions as Magnus and Tyler.

Tyler left his friend to do his job.

When Tyler reached the wolfkin cages, they were empty. He looked around and listened. Among the howling, he heard the sound of growling. It was coming from the direction of his father's yard.

Bow in hand, Tyler raced toward the sound. He took position behind the fence and peered to see what was happening.

Ruby had her hand on his father's cage door.

The moonlight lit her hair, highlighting the flame colors cascading over her shoulders. She looked slim and small, surrounded by four monstrous, growling beasts. They snarled at Tyler's father, who was standing in the middle of his cage. He looked like he wanted to both attack Ruby and back away as far as he could from the true monsters growling at him.

Tyler raised his bow, not sure if he could—or should—shoot his own father should he attack Ruby. Normally, as soon as he raised his bow and nocked an arrow, he felt cold calm settle over him. But this time, his emotions were jagged and he couldn't settle them.

He panted quietly, having a hard time catching his breath.

His vision blurred as he watched Ruby unlatch his father's cage.

The wolfkin's growls became lower, more aggressive as the creatures fanned around Ruby. Demanding. Unyielding. Deadly.

Tyler shifted his aim, not sure which one to target—his father or the wolfkin?

Ruby jerked open the cage door. She sprang out of the way and ran behind the wolfkin.

Father took a step toward the open door, then hesitated.

The wolfkin backed away, leaving room for Father to walk out. With their body movements, they were telling him to come out.

After a couple of heartbeats of hesitation, Father walked out of his cage. He stood hunched in the moonlight, the scraggly hairs on his back standing on end. He snarled, showing his fangs and bulging his oversized muscles like a dominant predator.

Father's howler form had always looked like a fierce monster, ready to devour anything in its path. But compared to the true wolfkin, he looked like a child playing at being a dog. He wouldn't have a chance against the true monsters.

But the wolfkin did not attack. They shepherded Father with the undeniable threat of death. They ushered him through the fence and into the broader yard.

Tyler backed into the shadows as they passed. He began to believe that perhaps it might actually be possible to leave Midnight Castle with his father and Ruby.

But he should have known better.

As soon as they were in the open yard, the wolfkin chased his father, nipping at his heels. Father ran off in the direction of the forest.

At first, Father ran because the wolfkin chased him. But the monsters only chased him long enough to get him to run in the right direction. At one point, Father turned to look back.

The wolfkin were no longer chasing him. Father slowed down and stopped. He stood there in the field, lit by moonlight. Tyler took comfort in knowing that the dried grass was long enough to hide him if he crouched.

Father stood taller than Tyler had seen him since he'd become a howler. He was free. He could go anywhere he wanted.

For a moment, Tyler could swear that his father saw him. He dared to hope that some part of his father recognized him.

Then his father turned back toward the forest and ran. As he did so, he stooped low.

Tyler watched his father running on all fours as he disappeared into the darkness of the forest.

CHAPTER 51

*I*t became faster to free the howlers after the first one. Tyler saw Ruby and the wolfkin get into a rhythm where she would open the cages and the wolfkin would chase the howlers until they headed toward the forest.

The howlers seemed to have an instinct to run into the forest the way a newborn turtle instinctively raced to the sea. The wolfkin seemed satisfied to just let them run without their supervision. Tyler guessed there were wolfkin just beyond the edge of the forest, ready to corral the howlers back to their den.

Tyler trotted over to where Ruby was working. He forced himself to shoulder his bow and arrow. He felt naked without his weapon in hand, but it wasn't good at close distance anyway.

He pulled out his knife. It was too small to do much, but he still felt better having it in his hand.

The wolfkin all watched him as he neared.

"Do you want me to open this cage or not?" asked Ruby.

She wasn't talking to Tyler. He marveled at how the

wolfkin controlled their killer instincts and turned back to her.

"I'll help," said Tyler. He wasn't sure if they would listen to him.

A silver wolfkin loped over to him and stood in front of the cage next to Tyler. Another wolfkin followed and stood on the other side of the cage door.

The sharp scent of the wild wolfkin mixed with the stench of the howler cages really brought home the magnitude of what Tyler was doing. He'd spent his entire life at the castle. He was about to leave everything and everyone he knew. His heritage. His future. All to live in the wild with these unnatural beasts.

His insides quivered at the thought, and his last meal wanted to come up.

But he wasn't about to leave everyone. He'd be with his father soon. His old friend was coming with him. And then there was this remarkable girl.

Another wolfkin walked toward them with a stiff gait. Magnus was beside him, carrying his leather healer's bag.

"His healing is remarkable," said Magnus. "I've never seen anything like it. And I swear he understands me. Who would have thought?"

There was a spark of excitement in his voice that Tyler hadn't heard in years. It gave him hope about what life might be like after Midnight Castle. *If* there was a life after.

Ruby and Tyler opened their separate cages.

The wolfkin snarled fiercely while the howlers backed away from the door. As soon as Tyler and Ruby were out of harm's way, the wolfkin snapped and bullied the howlers until they were running toward the forest.

Magnus and the injured wolfkin followed the howlers into the woods, moving at a slower pace. They'd be well on their way to the wolfkin den by the time the rest of them were finished here.

With Tyler on the team, the work progressed at double the speed after that. Good thing too, because it was a wonder that no one was out checking the cages with all this racket the howlers were making.

"We need to move faster," he said. "My men will come any moment, and I don't want them hurt."

"Someone's taking care of it," said Ruby.

"What do you mean?" Tyler felt cold inside thinking of his sleeping men and their families.

"Don't worry, I don't think it's an attack," she said as she opened another cage. "It doesn't seem to be Briar's style."

"What is it, then?" Tyler opened his cage and ran to the next.

"I'm not sure. But she's somehow keeping your hunters from coming here tonight."

"How?"

"I don't know the details. She's good at impersonations, though."

"That's supposed to trick *all* my men into—"

"*Who goes there?*"

A hunter stepped out into the moonlight along the edge of the yard. He had his bow aimed and his arrow nocked.

"What are you doing?" It was Clemens.

"It's me, Clemens." Tyler stepped into the moonlight.

He held his hands out to indicate to both Clemens and the wolfkin to hold back their attacks. Tyler realized too late that he should have extracted a promise from the wolfkin not to harm any person at all. They wouldn't have agreed—they were predators, after all—but he could have tried.

There was a tense moment when Clemens held his aim. Did he blame Tyler for Mathewson's death? What did he think of seeing Tyler freeing the howlers with wild wolfkin by his side? Did he wonder if these were the same beasts that killed Mathewson and the others?

The wolfkin all snarled at Clemens and tensed.

"Quiet down," Tyler growled, hoping the wolfkin would respect the command more that way.

The wolfkin quieted, although they still slowly fanned out around Clemens.

"What are you doing?" asked Clemens.

Tyler opened his mouth, not sure of what to say. He simply allowed the words to flow out of his mouth without thinking much about it.

"We can't do this forever, Clemens. We all know it. We'll all die one by one before the king is satisfied."

"We just caught three wild ones. The king must be satisfied with that."

"He's not. And he won't be until he has an army of wolfkin."

"An army? I thought he wanted them as pets."

Tyler shook his head. "He wants an army. We've lost men every full moon, and we've only managed to capture a few."

He didn't bother to say that most of them chose to be captured. He let Clemens grapple with what Tyler had just told him.

"Go back to bed, Clemens. In the morning, tell them I dismissed you from your duties for the night. Tell them you heard nothing. You're next in line now that Mathewson is gone. You can take over my position. It'll be a new life for you and your sons. You'd do a better job of it than me anyway."

Tyler could sense that he'd caught the man's imagination with the idea of becoming the royal huntsman. It was a hereditary position. Even if every member of the Huntsman's family died, Mathewson would have stepped in. But now, Mathewson was dead, leaving Clemens to be next in line.

"You can be proud to leave your heritage to your sons, Clemens. In time, they would be royal huntsmen."

"We're running out of time," whispered Ruby.

"Go, keep working." With his palms still out to Clemens, Tyler stepped between him and Ruby, making sure that Clemens didn't have a clear shot at her.

Ruby hesitantly walked to the next cage. Tyler made sure to move with her to block the arrow should Clemens shoot. This was between him and Clemens. Ruby shouldn't pay the price for that.

"These beasts will terrorize the village and kill everyone," said Clemens.

"They won't. They're going into the woods, and they'll stay there. The wolfkin have never come in to attack the village. We're the ones who've gone into their forest to hunt them, not the other way around."

"But the howlers—"

"Any one of us could become one tomorrow. You know that."

Clemens had worked for Tyler's father before Tyler took over. He and Mathewson had been by young Tyler's side when they first saw Tyler's father in howler form. Father had been pushed out of Sorcerer's Tower dazed and confused. Tyler didn't need to explain to Clemens about the punishments the Dark King could dole out when he was displeased.

Clemens lowered his bow with a sigh. "Your father was a good man."

Tyler nodded. "You'll be in charge after tonight. Take care of the men, Clemens."

Clemens hesitated. There were risks in lying to the king. But then again, it was just as risky to tell the truth.

Clemens finally nodded and disappeared into the shadows.

Tyler let out a long breath. There was no turning back now.

CHAPTER 52

Tyler ran to the next cage and let out the howlers as fast as he could. One after the other, he and Ruby freed the beasts. Some of them had been caged here since the Dark King first decided he wanted an army. Even though they never turned into full wolfkin, the king kept them anyway.

The yard had been getting quieter as the howlers vacated it. The ones who were left tried to make up for the quiet by howling as loudly as they could. Despite their fractured minds, they still understood that others were being set free, and they didn't want to be left behind.

Ruby opened a cage and let the last howler out. The wolfkin nipped and growled, directing the howler toward the forest.

Every other time, they'd herded the howler until his instincts took over. This time, though, the wolfkin continued to run into the field. They looked like they weren't coming back.

The silver wolfkin paused on the edge of the field of dried

grass while the others continued to run toward the forest. She looked back as though urging Ruby and Tyler to come.

Ruby ran along the empty cages toward her, looking over to wave Tyler to follow. He began to run after her, but a frantic barking behind him caught his attention.

Shadow raced between the rows of cages toward him at full speed.

Clemens must have untied him from the post outside the healer's cottage.

It was a gesture of goodwill. Shadow would not rest until he found Tyler, even if that meant roaming in the dangerous forest. As long as he was at Midnight Castle, they'd have a way of tracking down Tyler.

He frowned. As much as he wanted Shadow with him, a dog was not a good fit for Tyler's new life.

Shadow would be surrounded by wolfkin. They were massive compared to a dog. They were wild killers who would look at Shadow as both runt and meat. No dog deserved that.

Still, he supposed it was no more dangerous than Tyler going to the wolfkin's den. Ruby had told him that it was a place where both he and Magnus could live. A place with other people. Tyler couldn't imagine what such a place would be like, but he wasn't committed to staying there if it wasn't to his liking.

No matter. It didn't look like Shadow was interested in Tyler's opinion anyway. Despite the dangers of the forest and the wolfkin, Shadow ran right to Tyler's side, as he always had.

"You crazy dog."

Tyler allowed himself a small smile. He bent down and rubbed Shadow's ear as the dog jumped and licked Tyler's face.

His smile froze, though, when he saw a red glow behind the kennels. Tyler stood up, trying to see if it was a fire.

Guards ran into view, their shiny armor reflecting flames from their torches. It was the king's guards.

Beside them, Clemens pointed to Tyler. The hunter must have caught the king before he went back to bed.

Tyler reeled from the betrayal.

He'd grown up among the hunters. They'd always been loyal to his father, and Tyler had thought to him as well.

But he must have sorely underestimated how angry Clemens would be to see the beasts that killed his friends run free. Tyler mentally kicked himself for not seeing that Clemens would gain the position of royal huntsman whether or not he let Tyler go. Now, he would gain the king's favor and start his new position having already proved himself.

Tyler spun and was about to run to Ruby when he saw the cages near her were also flickering with torchlight.

Ruby saw the guards coming toward her at the same time he did. She and the silver wolfkin turned and raced toward the forest.

The guards yelled and gave chase.

Tyler changed directions to avoid running into the stream of guards chasing Ruby. He cut through the rows of empty cages, weaving as fast as he could toward the forest.

CHAPTER 53

*T*yler couldn't let the king's guards catch Ruby. But there were too many of them for him to dive into a fight. He could only hope that she could outrun them to the forest.

Once they were in the woods, he and Ruby would have a better chance of survival. He'd be surprised if any of the guards had ever set foot in those woods. And on a night like this, their heads would be full of stories of what could happen in there.

Tyler raced through the field of dried grass with Shadow at his heels. Despite his own set of guards chasing him, Tyler kept an eye on Ruby as she ran.

The silver wolfkin stayed by her side even though she could have far outpaced Ruby. That gave Tyler some reassurance.

He raced toward the forest as fast as he could. Almost there. Once he reached the woods, there were many places to hide.

Tyler glanced to where he expected Ruby to be. She wasn't there.

He slowed and turned to look.

Ruby had shifted direction. Two horsemen had caught up to her and were corralling her toward the guards.

She weaved and feinted, forcing the horsemen to almost collide. She was taking advantage of the one thing she had over the horsemen—her ability to change directions quickly. The horsemen couldn't turn anywhere nearly as fast as she could.

But they didn't need to. The guards were almost on her.

Shadow barked a frantic warning. At first, Tyler thought he was barking for Ruby. But as the dog continued to bark at him, Tyler realized that he was warning Tyler of his own pursuers. They were getting too close for comfort.

Tyler was almost at the edge of the forest. He made a split-second decision to race the few steps to the closest tree.

"Go!" He pointed into the woods and injected as much command as he could into his voice.

Shadow, trained from birth to run into the woods when commanded, raced on.

Tyler jumped onto the tree and grabbed the lowest branch. He climbed to lie in wait for game to come near. As soon as he settled onto a branch, his bow was in his hands with the arrow nocked.

Ruby was surrounded by guards.

Anyone else would have given up, but not her. She stood her ground and fought as fiercely as a wolverine. She must know that there was no chance of surviving capture, not after what happened tonight. It was fight or die.

His breath caught as he watched her. She spun, kicking the nearest guard as he came at her. The torchlight gave Tyler a glimpse of her red cloak as it spun with her movements, looking like swirling blood in the night as she moved.

She was full of power and grace, spinning from one enemy to the other under the moonlight.

The silver wolfkin spooked the horses. Baring her teeth and snarling, she pushed horses and guards away from Ruby.

The horses reared in fright. Tyler knew from experience that a horse would bolt from wolfkin as soon as possible.

Their riders fought to control them. The horses circled a couple of times, fighting their riders and kicking in panic. They threw their riders off and raced back to the castle.

The wolfkin didn't bother to attack the fallen horsemen. Instead, she attacked the guards closest to Ruby.

The wolfkin could easily tear men to pieces—nobody knew that better than Tyler. But she didn't. She seemed almost careful not to kill them, although she had no qualms about hurting them.

Tyler had his own fight to attend to. The guards were almost to his tree. He let out a slow breath, taking aim. The cool wind from the forest tugged at his tunic as though the woods were breathing.

The guards ran down the dry field with their torches. There was about a dozen of them coming after him.

The king's guards were in armor and palace finery. That armor looked good in the castle, but it was clumsy and mostly for pageantry. Could he use that to his advantage?

Tyler swung his aim at Clemens, who was leading the chase. For a moment, he indulged in the fantasy of shooting his betrayer, just as he had as a lad.

How many times had he pretended to shoot Clemens as a boy? Clemens had even shown him how to aim right at his chest. Then, telling outlandish stories of hunts, he'd shown young Tyler how to make knots for snares.

Tyler moved his aim to the nearest guard. Even though the guards looked inhuman in their armor, he knew that was mostly designed to frighten and intimidate. He'd supped enough times with the king's guards to know several of them by name.

He shifted his aim to the torch held by the nearest guard. Being careful to angle his shot so as to avoid setting someone on fire, he loosed his arrow.

The torch flew out of the guard's hand, landing on the grass behind him.

The dried grass caught on fire.

As Tyler had expected, the forest took care of itself. The wind from the woods was just enough to keep the flames moving away from the forest.

The guards couldn't ignore a fire. Nobody wanted to be trapped in a metal suit near raging flames. They tried to stomp it out, but it quickly grew.

Tyler shot another torch out of a guard's hand. It fell and caught fire in a new area. The flames ate the dried grass and instantly spread.

Several of the guards began running toward the castle for reinforcements. They couldn't ignore a fire so close to the castle.

Tyler nocked another arrow. This time, he aimed it at the mass of guards around Ruby and the wolfkin.

The girl and beast were holding their own against the guards, but they were far outnumbered. They also couldn't run while they fought. It was just a matter of time before reinforcements arrived.

He aimed for a torch and let his arrow fly. His aim was true, and the grass near the guards caught on fire.

Another shot, and there was enough of a distraction to let Ruby and her wolfkin run toward the forest.

The guards were too busy running from the fire to chase. Those few who might still have been inclined to catch them weren't about to run into the forest in the middle of the night all by themselves.

Tyler waited until he was sure Ruby would be safe. Then

he swung his bow over his shoulder and hopped down from his branch.

As soon as his feet touched the ground, he raced into the forest.

CHAPTER 54

*R*uby woke stiff and tired. The sunlight streamed through the linen curtains of the arched window. Her bed was an enormous four-poster, and she was wrapped in silk sheets that felt like water flowing over her skin.

It took her a moment to figure out where she was. Her head was foggy, and her muscles ached. Then last night's rescue and escape from Midnight Castle came back to her.

Tyler.

He'd come with her. He'd helped release the howlers.

He'd kissed her.

Ruby stroked her lip in wonder. This was the first time she'd had a chance to think about that. It was the oddest feeling—a mix of being nervous, excited, embarrassed, and obsessed. It felt fragile and private, yet she wanted to tell everyone about it. At the same time, she was sure she'd shrivel in embarrassment if she talked about it.

She rubbed her face. Her grandmother had always told her to be bold and confident, to draw the line where she wanted it and not where others demanded. But Gran had never given her lessons on girly things like kissing. Not that she wanted her grandmother to give her those kinds of lessons.

Gran.

Ruby tossed off the luxurious blanket. There were slippers laid out for her and a thick robe draped over the foot of the bed.

Wolfkin certainly lived well. Not at all the grimy cave that she'd envisioned for their den.

Being a shy girl steeped in wonder over her first kiss was fine for most village girls, but she was in the Wolfkin den, surrounded by beasts that could tear her to pieces. She had to find her grandmother and Tyler.

A beautiful dress hung on an armoire. It looked perfectly tailored for her and was made of material so airy that it looked like violet froth. Below that were her hunter's clothes that she'd worn for days. They were clean now and folded in a neat pile on a footstool.

As much as she wanted to wear the dress, she threw on her old clothes. This was not the time to be frivolous. She needed to be prepared for anything, and she couldn't do it in a frothy dress.

There was a knock on her door.

Ruby froze, not sure if everyone in the mansion knew she was here.

Last night, they'd run, then walked for most of the long night. She didn't know how the wolfkin ever found their mansion. For hours, every tree and rock, every hill and gully looked the same. Then, suddenly, the walls of the mansion loomed ahead of them.

"Ruby, it's me, Gran." The door opened, and there was her grandmother, holding a basket.

She looked just as Ruby remembered—silver hair pulled back into a bun, her trim body looking fit, her jewel eyes seeing everything.

Ruby ran into her arms. Gran was mostly steel and muscle, but she had a warmth to her that always made Ruby feel protected and loved.

"You did well, child." Gran stroked Ruby's hair.

"I've missed you, Gran." Ruby kissed her on the cheek.

Gran squeezed her. "I looked everywhere for you. I was afraid I'd lost you."

"And I'm glad you're a person again." Ruby smiled. "It's better to have you hug me than to lick my face. I didn't know you worked with witches."

"I usually don't. It was worth it, though." She rubbed her cheek on Ruby's hair.

"You saved me, you know. I couldn't have survived the castle without your training. I dreamt about you training me all the time."

"You saved yourself. As a true granddaughter of mine should." Gran took a step back and scanned Ruby from the tip of her head to her toes. She seemed satisfied that all Ruby's limbs were still in place.

"So, you recruited the Huntsman." She sounded impressed. It wasn't easy to impress Gran.

"Is he all right? Have you seen him?"

Gran smiled. "I'll take you to him."

Ruby followed Gran down the stairs.

This was the first time she'd seen the mansion in daylight. Last night, when they'd finally arrived, she was too tired to notice much and there was only a single candle for her to find her room. Now, she finally got to see the mansion in all its glory.

It was the kind of place that casually showed spectacular wealth. The stairs were wide with gold filigree decorating the banister. The rug on the stairs was of the richest colors, and all around her was sunlight. The ceiling had an unusual feature that let the sunlight into the mansion.

"It must be amazing in the rain," said Ruby as she stared up at the skylights.

"Specially built so that the full moon would bathe the main rooms," said Gran.

"It must be quite a party on full moons here."

"The full moon has power. This mansion respects and honors it as much as it can."

Downstairs, the front doors were wide open, giving Ruby a view of the walkway. In front of the doors were two men— both tall and broad and outlined in the sunshine. Ruby knew without seeing their faces that they were Tyler and Magnus.

Her heart sped up and her hands became moist. She wasn't this nervous before a fight. How could she be so nervous to face a man?

"...remarkable. I'm having a hard time believing what I'm seeing." Magnus sounded excited and alive.

"Mmm." Tyler sounded far away.

As Ruby and Gran approached, Ruby could see what they were looking at. The walkway bordered the flower garden on one side and the howler area on the other side where she'd seen the howlers chained on her last visit. This time, though, the poles had nothing but empty chains attached to them.

Ahead, the mansion gates were open and the last of the howlers were running out. Behind them were several wolfkin. After seeing them in action all night, Ruby recognized that they were herding the howlers.

"Where are they going?" asked Ruby.

The men turned to look at her. Ruby couldn't help but wonder how Tyler would look at her if she had put on that dress in her bedroom. Her cheeks warmed.

He smiled, looking like he knew what she was thinking, even though he couldn't possibly know.

"They're taking the howlers out for a run," said Magnus.

"That's something we never could do at the castle. Too dangerous by far. But none of them dare to misbehave here with the wolfkin nipping at them. Amazing."

"They're being allowed to roam free in the woods for a few hours," said Tyler. His voice sounded a bit thick, with a hint of suppressed emotion.

He seemed far away as he smiled. "My father hasn't been out of his cage in years. When I saw the howlers chained in the yard, I wondered how this was better than having him in a cage at the castle."

"Now we know." Magnus nodded his approval. "I can't wait to get a good look at them. My guess is that they are much healthier, possibly less aggressive, but I wouldn't bet on that."

Gran pointed to the howler yard. "Exercise time also gives families a chance to clean up the holding area."

Between the poles, people were sweeping, exchanging the dirty water and food bowls for clean ones. A man with a large leather belt with tools hanging on it was checking the collars and leather strips hanging on the chains. He filed down sharp edges and replaced the torn strips.

Another man went around oiling the leather. That would keep the straps supple and chafe as little as possible.

"They get good care here," said Ruby.

"Yes," whispered Tyler. "They do." He cleared his throat and took a deep breath.

"You all right?" asked Magnus.

"Never better." Tyler gave him a faint smile. "I just didn't think my father would ever..." He shrugged. "This isn't exactly paradise, but it's better than what he had. He's not a monster here."

"This is all temporary," said Gran.

"Until what?" Tyler frowned.

"Until they can fix them, of course," Gran said like it was obvious.

"Fix them?" asked Tyler. "How? It was black magic that turned them this way."

"The moon and the forest have their own magic, and so do the wolfkin. We have a plan."

"What plan?" asked Magnus.

"No need for you to worry your pretty little head over it." Gran smiled at the healer. "You'll know if the plan works. I'm afraid it might take some time, though."

"I'll need to worry my pretty little head over it if it involves me running around, trying to stanch the damage done by dark sorcery," said Magnus. "I've had enough of that to last me a lifetime."

"This isn't Midnight Castle," said Gran as she walked down the steps into the flower garden. "The wolfkin have their own ways."

"You talk like you're not one of them," said Tyler. "You were the silver wolf from last night, aren't you?"

"I'm Silver, Ruby's grandmother. Pleased to meet you, Huntsman."

"I'm no longer the royal huntsman."

"No, now you're our huntsman. We hunt too, you know." Gran smiled, showing her even teeth.

Gran began to cut stems of flowers and place them in her basket.

"Those are beautiful," Ruby said. "Can you take them?"

"Where do you think I get my night flowers? With the night becoming so long, the normal flowers are no longer in fashion. But these will be the height of fashion as soon as I tell my customers that they bloom at night."

She held up a closed flower. It was exotic, and Ruby could smell it from the steps.

"Help me pick them, Ruby. Grab that basket over there.

We'll take them home and put them in water before breakfast."

"Home?" Ruby hadn't known what to expect, but picking flowers and going home for breakfast had not been on the list of possibilities. She glanced at Tyler.

"Oh, he stays." Gran took a deep sniff of a blue and yellow flower. "Not to worry, though—we'll be back soon. I come here regularly to replenish my flower supply."

"Ruby just escaped from Midnight Castle and is a fugitive," said Tyler. "They'll be looking for her."

"They'll be looking for *you*," said Gran. "And your friend. And all the howlers and wolfkin that they expect to be running around town. Will they be looking for a young woman at the market who is helping her grandmother sell flowers?" She shrugged. "Unlikely. Besides, they'll have their hands full. There's more going on in the Kingdom of Midnight than meets the eye."

"Oh, Gran, please don't start in on the Wild Wars again," Ruby said. "It's embarrassing."

"Then get to work and fill up that basket before I embarrass you even more in front of your man."

"He's not my man, Gran," Ruby whispered as she quickly filled her basket.

"Oh, he will be soon enough, if he's not already. I predict, say...in two days, when we come back to replenish the flower supply."

"*Gran.*"

Tyler's lips quirked in what looked suspiciously like a smile. "I look forward to seeing you and your lovely granddaughter then, madam."

"Perhaps you can teach Ruby how to move about in the woods without sounding like a falling tree. I never did have enough time to teach her the art of silence."

Ruby's cheeks were definitely feeling hot.

"Until then," said Gran as she walked down the path toward the gates, "make yourself useful so that the wolfkin will take good care of you. You earned their respect last night, which is no easy feat. Now, you just need to keep it."

"We'll do our best, madam," said Magnus.

"Ruby, kiss your man goodbye and come along. It's long past time to go home."

Ruby looked at Tyler like a rabbit caught in a snare. But Tyler didn't seem to mind.

Without hesitation, he stepped over and leaned in toward her. Ruby almost dropped her flowers but managed to keep everything together. She was Silver's granddaughter, and she could fight crazed howlers and befriend dogs trained to kill. She could handle a little kiss.

She stood on her toes and met Tyler halfway.

<u>Midnight Tales novels</u>

Cinder & the Prince of Midnight

Ruby & the Huntsman of Midnight

Briar & the Dreamers of Midnight

Hansel & the Witch of Midnight

Don't miss a new story from Susan EE!

Sign up to hear about them at:

www. S u s a n E E .com

Aim your phone camera at this image to see the Midnight Tales novels

www.ingramcontent.com/pod-product-compliance
Lightning Source LLC
Chambersburg PA
CBHW022108240626
47153CB00007B/2284